# HOUND of the BASKERVILLES

## An Erotic Tale

# Praise for *Hound of the Baskervilles*

"At once decadently gothic and refreshingly modern, *Hound of the Baskervilles* offers a moving reimagining of the Holmes/Watson relationship. Featuring an alluring, sensuously-rendered cast of dubious characters—including witches, escaped murderers, druids, and shadowy creatures too strange to define—the novel is darkly theatrical, and at times terror-inducing, in its literary vision. From the opening murder of a victim 'buggered to death' to its orgiastic denouement, the novel showcases McOmber as an author who masterfully interweaves the beauty and barbarity of sex: the un-uttered secrets and yearnings that underpin it, the monstrosities we think ourselves to be—and the very real monsters we come up against. Every page is alive with murky vitality; McOmber moves us from scene to candle-lit scene, where redemption—or annihilation—is only a lover's breath away. Shadows fawn and fornicate in the spaces between the lines of McOmber's exquisite prose. Monsters of delirious creativity take the plot in startling new directions, and we follow Watson through a macabre trail of murders to an ending as shocking as it is poetic—and where the boundaries between man and beast blur. The final chapters are a fever dream of priapic vision: presenting cosmic horror—and beauty—in Wildean excess."

—Phoenix Alexander, the Jay Kay Klein and Doris Klein Librarian for Science Fiction and Fantasy, UC Riverside

"McOmber's haunting variation on the Holmes-Watson mythos is a dark, unsettling rumination on queer desire. Unabashedly homoerotic, and steeped in Folk Horror."

—Craig Laurance Gidney, author of *A Spectral Hue and The Nectar of Nightmares*

"An important voice in the genre."
—Becky Spratford, *Booklist*

"A fascinating portrait...the unexpected twists are sure to keep readers hooked. Holmes fans ... will enjoy this supernatural mystery."
—*Publishers Weekly*

"A haunted dreamscape of gothic imagery and erotic encounters. Readers will be left stunned, aroused, and more likely than not, newly entranced fans of McOmber's chimerical pen."
—Tom Cardamone, author of Lambda-Award-winner *Green Thumb*

## For *Fantasy Kit*

"Adam McOmber's stories are the work of an architect and master illusionist. He constructs fairy tales that twist into labyrinths, labyrinths that open up gloriously into new myths—and always, as if just under the page, is the thump and flow of blood, the pulsing, hidden desire of the human heart."
—James Tadd Adcox, author of *Does Not Love* and *Repetition*

"We can't help but marvel: how fantastically complex this is, how chillingly scrambled, and yet how poetically immaculate, how jarring, how sad. What feels like genius in this story is its ability to craft a culminating situation that feels so nearly impossible to parse and yet so piercingly coherent."
—Zach Schwab, *The Brooklyn Rail*

## For *Jesus and John*

"The story humanizes characters that often seem untouchable ... [This] adventure leaves the reader with much to think about, inspiring interpretation and reflection long after it ends."

—*ForeWord Reviews*

"There are many occult horror novels out there, but Jesus and John's fully articulated gnostic horror puts it in a class all its own—as if Lovecraft had rewritten the Nag Hammadi codices. Beautifully written, heretical, and profoundly humane, this is a book about destabilizing one's entire sense of reality and revealing the unreal lurking within."

—Brian Evenson, author of *Song for the Unraveling of the World*

## For *My House Gathers Desires*

"An otherworldly collection of tales rich with mystery, suspense, and eroticism."

—*Kirkus Review*

"If Adam McOmber didn't make it clear enough in his first two books of fiction that his imagination knows no bounds, his new collection *My House Gathers Desires* is fresh and certain evidence. His pantry of interests is on full display, is in full play, as he navigates gender and sexuality through the lens of dark dreams, science fiction, medical quackery, and fairy tales."

—Brian Leung, *Lambda Literary*

## For *The White Forest*

"Commandingly erudite and imaginative, McOmber meshes myth, the occult, and 19th-century technological advances in an uncanny and captivating gothic tale."

—Donna Seaman, *Booklist*

## For *This New & Poisonous Air*

"Eerie, sorrowful, and disquieting, McOmber's exquisite tales of taboo longings brilliantly illuminate the gossamer divide between loss and love, madness and reason, death and life."

—Donna Seaman, *Booklist*

Published by Lethe Press | lethepressbooks.com

ISBN: 978-1-59021-519-7



Typesetting: Ryan Vance

# HOUND of the BASKERVILLES

## An Erotic Tale

Adam McOmber

# 1

*October 14th, 19—*

*Baskerville Hall.*

*Black ship upon a blacker sea.*

*(And am I not adrift as well? Am I not about to drown?)*

*What follows are my private notes. Fragments and impressions from which I'll gather a daily report for Sherlock Holmes.*

*A case of forgery in London has delayed Holmes himself.*

*Or that is what he tells me, at least...*

*I've been sent ahead to Dartmoor, to an ancient manor house that stands at the edge of the great bogland known as the Grimpen Mire. There, I'm to meet our client, a Dr. Mortimer, this very morning (if I can rightly use the word "morning" here. For no light penetrates the low ceiling of the clouds. It's as if there has never been a sun).*

*I frequently pause to jot these notes. Holmes implores me to do so, lest I forget anything of import. He believes I do not recognize what is important. And yet, after what happened so recently in London, I know I can say the same of him with some certainty.*

*I will not linger in the past, however.*

*I've promised myself as much.*

*Here then...*

*

I catch my first glimpse of Baskerville Hall from a distance on the train to Devonshire and then from the four-wheeled wagonette that conveys me along the moorland road. A very old man, the Baskerville groom, drives the wagonette. And though he is wrapped in a cowled gray shawl, he trembles in the autumn chill. When we are near the house, he raises his whip to point. "There, sir," he says. "Baskerville Hall."

The house, a heavy block of black granite, sits in a low depression beneath a cragged and melancholy rise. Two weather-bitten towers extend from the central block like fingers from a desiccated hand. And all around, a dark and creeping ivy, out from which stare the hall's many mullioned windows.

As the wagonette passes through the grove of stunted oak and storm-wracked fir before the iron gates, I think this house, with all its curious murk and shadow, is most certainly an object from a dream.

But who should dream a thing like this?

Perhaps the dark landscape of the moor itself has fallen into reverie—the mottled bramble and standing stones, the Neolithic tombs all covered with lichen.

*Here is a noisy, foaming river.*

*Here, three red cows near a crumbling wall.*

*I admit I am not in the right mind for this endeavor.*

*Recent events (of which I will not speak) have caused me again to rely upon an opiate to quell my nerves. The bottle of laudanum weighs heavily in the pocket of my overcoat.*

*From a medical perspective, there is no shame in ingesting opium, of course, but I fear the frequent doses will make me less observant.*

*Holmes is so fastidious in gathering details, especially in the initial hours of a case. He tells me that, as time moves on, the evidence tends to hide itself away like a slug beneath a rock. But in the beginning, clues lay more fully in the open.*

I am greeted at the weathered entryway of Baskerville Hall not by Dr. Mortimer, who, according to his letter, is residing at the house to care for the ailing baronet, Sir Henry Baskerville, but by a young man who looks as if he might work in the stable yards. He is fiercely handsome in a rustic way, black-eyed and strong-boned with whiskers on his chin. I cannot stop myself from gazing down his strapping length—his lithe shoulders, sinewed arms, and pale and calloused hands. And lower still, the weight that hangs just beneath the fly of his trousers.

If I am honest, he has the look of one of the young men I met near Piccadilly during my recent difficulties. Telegraph boys used to provide a modicum of comfort, but since the Cleveland Street scandal, I must rely on the young men who linger near the Criterion.

I cannot help but think of a certain youth known as "Tom the Horse" (so-called for reasons that become evident the moment he lowers his drawers). He's a wiry fellow, a boxer in the bare-knuckle fights, and I have paid to meet with him and his ruby-headed cock on several occasions. He tells me he appreciates my aging soldier's body. I do not believe him, of course. He's most likely in love with one of the other boys at the Criterion, or even a girl for that matter.

But now and again, I allow myself the possibility of a dream.

The young servant at Baskerville Hall barely glances in my direction before leading me by lamplight through the paneled foyer to a sitting room where I am asked to wait for the appearance of Dr. Mortimer.

The room is comfortable enough with high raftered ceilings and velvet club chairs. A somber-looking stag's head stares down from a spot above the Baskerville coat of arms. I am glad to see a fire has been lit, and I extend my hands toward it, rubbing my palms dryly. I can already feel the dampness of the moor evaporating. I suppose it's my age that makes me so prone to a chill. That and my rather lagging health stems from the fact that little in my life has occurred in the manner it should.

I've lived an odd bachelor's existence on Baker Street for far too long. And I've put all my faith in someone who proves, time and again, that he has no faith in me.

Such experiences change a man, do they not? (A trajectory is altered.)

I am no longer the brave soldier who fought as part of the Fifth Northumberland in Candahar. Or even the wounded veteran who arrived in London with a bit of hope still left in his heart.

Men glance at me far less in the thoroughfare.

And I, in turn, try to glance less at them as well.

How embarrassing if Holmes saw with what frequency I digress in these pages. And yet I wonder: would he feel somehow satisfied?

I have almost nodded off in the parlor, likely due to the effects of opium when I sense a presence in the room. I open my eyes and will myself not to reach for the revolver concealed in my jacket pocket. Holmes told me I must be diligent about carrying arms on this trip, saying the lonely hills of Dartmoor may prove a dangerous territory indeed.

Standing before me in the warm glow of the firelight is a well-made man of late middle age, broad in the way the country can make a man broad. He wears a refined woolen suit, gray in color, that might have been purchased in one of the better shops on Monmouth Street, and he walks, due to some unseen imperfection, with the aid of a bulbous-headed cane.

"Dr. Watson," he says, extending a well-manicured hand. His voice has a pleasant timbre that puts me immediately at ease.

"Indeed," I say, rising to greet him.

"I'm Dr. James Mortimer, County Practitioner. Thank you for coming. I understand we were both surgeons in another life."

"Many lives ago, it often seems to me."

He offers a thin smile and asks me to sit while he rings the bell for tea. The dark-haired servant boy who greeted me at the door soon arrives with a cart. I try not to follow his every move or sniff the air for his musk when he draws near.

As the tea is poured, a wave of mild dizziness passes

over me. (Black ship upon a blacker sea... and now the ship rocks to and fro). Perhaps the spell is brought on by the presence of the young man. Or, more likely, it's merely time for another dose of laudanum.

"Sherlock Holmes has been detained," I say to Dr. Mortimer, wiping at my brow with a handkerchief. "But he's taken a keen interest in the case described in your letter. He asked me to gather as many facts as I could. I'm sorry that he's—"

"No need to apologize. I've read quite a number of your pieces in The Strand and understand your working methods well enough."

I nod, satisfied. My writing is the single pride left to me.

"I'm afraid my letter was rather too delicate in its descriptions," Dr. Mortimer says. "The actual events are of a much darker nature."

"And pressing as well, I gather." I take a sip of strong black tea.

"Pressing indeed."

"Let's start at the beginning, if you don't mind. The death..."

Dr. Mortimer shifts his grip on the cane that rests against his thigh. "As you know, my patient Charles Baskerville met his end in the Yew Alley behind the house. He'd been living with his beloved cousin, Henry for some years. The hall is their ancestral home, you understand. And Henry Baskerville still resides here. I tended to both of them for a disorder of the nerves. Of course, I tell you this in confidence as a fellow physician."

"Of course," I say. "And could you describe for me the condition of the body?"

"It's a distasteful thing."

I take another sip of tea.

"Sir Charles was found dead and naked amongst the yew trees by the servant boy called Barrymore, the one you met upon your arrival. The murder must have happened sometime after midnight, during an hour when everyone else had gone off to bed. Barrymore discovered the scene in the early morning just as he was setting about his daily chores. There were bruises on Sir Charles's neck and scratches all about. But that's not what killed him."

"What did kill him then?" I ask.

"He was—by all apparent evidence—buggered to death."

I set my cup down rather too firmly in its saucer.

"Flayed, Dr. Watson, from his nethers. Lying in a great pool of his own blood. And now, of course, Henry Baskerville's nervous condition has deteriorated. That's why I've agreed to stay at the house with him. Sir Henry fears the Baskerville Curse took his cousin. And he believes the curse will now, in turn, take him. For he is next in line to inherit the hall."

"The curse, yes," I say. "You mentioned that in your letter. Why does he believe it was this so-called curse and not some manmade plot?"

"Because of the other piece of evidence I have yet to mention—a series of footprints found near the body."

"That of a man or woman?"

"No," Dr. Mortimer replies grimly. "The footprints of an enormous hound."

*

*Here, I shall make myself pause. I so often lose my way in note-taking such as this due to the manner in which I've trained myself to produce pieces for* The Strand. *Readers want stories, I am told. But Holmes himself does not. He appreciates details, yes. "Facts," as he calls them. But he does not care for what he deems the tired spinnings of Romance. "The novel, Watson, is a simple machine made for the unimaginative mind. I am not a man who requires the trappings of a scene." And so, I will limit myself in this telling. As I have often limited myself before. For what is the point of telling stories to a man who does not—and never will—listen?*

*In brief, then, for Holmes: The moor is very sparsely inhabited, according to Dr. Mortimer. There are only two other dwellings in the vicinity of Baskerville Hall. The first, called Laughter Hall, is occupied by a mysterious recluse and inventor. And the second, a rather dilapidated medieval cottage known as Merripit House, is being rented by a naturalist called Stapleton and his eccentric sister. Also of note: some fourteen miles to the south is the convict prison of Princetown. Several weeks ago, a known murderer and possible madman by the name of Seldon (the convicted perpetrator of the ghastly Notting Hill murders) escaped the prison and is thought to be hiding somewhere on the moor.*

*Before I push ahead, I should also describe the nature of the aforementioned Baskerville Curse. I am quite certain Holmes will care nothing for this rather shocking old tale, as he places all such talk in the same fanciful category as the novel. But the legend seems of some import to Dr. Mortimer. And it is certainly of significance to Henry Baskerville himself.*

*

The story of the curse dates back to the seventeenth century, during the time of the Great Rebellion, when a certain Hugo Baskerville, a Royalist general, held lordly sway over the already crumbling hall upon the moor. Hugo was said to be a godless man with a predilection for simple fare—namely peasant boys—and when he was in his wine, he would take his black horse down to the village of Grimpen and steal a wide-eyed youth from the cobbled streets. The boys stumbled back to the village days later, bearing secrets (stories shared only amongst themselves) of the horrors they had witnessed at Baskerville Hall. It was witchcraft, they said, for Sir Hugo Baskerville was a sorcerer. He painted his naked body with arcane symbols and summoned devils from the yellow air. The devils took many terrible shapes—a great lizard with a flickering tongue and a black he-goat with a cock so long it dragged upon the flagstones. But worst of all was the enormous hound. The Hound of the Baskervilles, the boys called it. A melancholy beast that would clamber and claw its way up from a fissure in the earth. It had molten black eyes and a mouthful of yellow teeth. And it whined and howled and seemed as if it wanted to flee its own existence. As if its soul was a great and prickling thorn stuck deep inside its breast. But Sir Hugo would not allow the Hound to flee. He held the creature in his sorcerer's gaze. Sometimes the beast appeared in the form of a dog. But at other times, it looked more like a gigantic hair-covered man. For that was the way with hellhounds, the boys said. They could not maintain a single shape. They were all rawness and trembling and sorrow, like the bodies, left unnamed in the Garden because Adam could not bear to look at them.

And Hugo would lay with this Hound of the Baskervilles, compelling the peasant boys to bear witness to his depravity. The Hound began as a dog and then turned into a man and then into something in between, all the while screaming and howling with Hugo writhing beneath. The Hound shook the very walls of the house with its forceful thrusts as if to bring Baskerville Hall to the ground. Watching all of this, the peasant boys would fold their trembling hands and pray. But prayers grew quickly lost in those winding torchlit halls. And the boys would eventually lose their senses too. There was no room for Heaven at Baskerville Hall. There was only one Hell layered upon the next.

Then one day, according to legend, Hugo Baskerville no longer came to the village of Grimpen. He was seen no more walking the desolate roads. Nor did he call to his servants from the black towers of his house. When the barristers arrived to investigate, they found the rooms of Baskerville Hall well ordered. There was no sign of struggle. And certainly, no body to be discovered. The peasant boys of the village said in hushed tones that the miserable Hound had finally murdered the villain and dragged his corpse back down into the foul, black fissure in the earth. From that day forth, the Hound was said to return and punish all Baskerville men who dared lay claim to the rambling hall upon the moor. They are forever made to atone for Hugo's vile trespasses. And theirs is always an atonement of blood.

The story of the curse, as told, leaves an odd residue in the parlor. A vibration of sorts. As if a bell has been rung.

Dr. Mortimer strokes the head of his cane.

I sit with my hands folded in my lap.

The young servant, Barrymore, stands in the shadows of the foyer. He's been listening intently as Dr. Mortimer recounted the legend. I have no idea what his eavesdropping might mean. But, of course, my thoughts don't matter here. Holmes has often told me not to theorize as it interferes with his own processes.

"Charles Baskerville wasn't merely a patient," Dr. Mortimer says after a prolonged pause. "He was also my friend. And I am sorry he is gone. But his death does not cause me to call upon Sherlock Holmes."

I clear my throat. "What other cause?"

"I have reason to think Henry Baskerville's belief that he will be the next to die is not mere fantasy."

"What reason?"

"A message," Dr. Mortimer replies. "Delivered late last week." He reaches into the breast pocket of his jacket and produces a folded piece of parchment.

As he makes to hand it to me, a terrible scream erupts from the upper stories of the house. A horrid, fearful sound that trembles the air about us.

Dizziness rocks me once again.

The boy in the foyer produces a low moaning sound.

"Dear God," Dr. Mortimer says, standing from his seat. "It's Sir Henry. Come, Dr. Watson, we must attend!"

The screams rise again. High and unmanly.

And as we rush toward the darkened stair, Baskerville Hall seems to gather its shadows before us, ready to open a black curtain and begin the play.

# 2

"It moved, Dr. Mortimer! Of its own infernal accord!" Henry Baskerville, thin and pale, no more than twenty-five years of age, sits upright in an ornate bed, sheets pulled to his neck, gesturing at a shape in the corner of the room.

The shape in question, incredibly, appears to be a man-sized wooden mannequin slumped in a cane back chair. The mannequin has no eyes or mouth. The whole of its head is carved from a single piece of smooth and featureless oak. Its body, however, is fully articulated—brass jointed shoulders, wrists, knees, etc. And most shockingly, the mannequin is possessed with a large curved phallus, some ten inches in length, made from what appears to be an elephant's tusk.

"Sir Henry," Dr. Mortimer says, breathless from our run. "We have discussed this very issue on several occasions."

"I do not care how many times we've discussed it, James," Henry Baskerville says. "I know what I saw."

Dr. Mortimer shakes his head. "The mannequin is a totem. And a cure. Your cousin understood that well enough."

"And my cousin is dead," Sir Henry says, raking his long auburn hair back from his rather handsome Celtic brow. "My dear, beloved Charles. Dead because he did not question the unnatural goings-on in this house."

"The mannequin is not unnatural," Dr. Mortimer offers in a soothing tone. "It is of my own devising. Well-tested in previous cases with men of your... nature."

"I awoke and saw it lurking there by the window." Sir Henry gestures at a spot some ten paces from the chair. "It was looking at me. Then it took a step toward me. And that's when I began to scream. By the time you arrived, it had returned to its place in the chair."

Dr. Mortimer lights a lamp on the side table near the mannequin and peers down at the wooden form. "This is Dr. John Watson, by the way. I told you he'd be arriving today."

Henry Baskerville regards me rather starkly. "You work with Sherlock Holmes?"

"I do, Sir Henry."

"And he has agreed to come here? He will protect me?"

"Holmes has been detained in London, but he assures me he will arrive within the week."

"That will be too late!" Sir Henry covers his face with a trembling hand. "I do not want to die."

"None of us want that," Dr. Mortimer replies. "We shall all work to protect you. Never fear."

"The powers of evil are exalted upon the moor," Sir Henry says. "That witch at Merripit House has affected the bog in some way. I know it. The mire itself grows restless."

I gaze out the bedroom window at the dimly painted landscape stretching beneath a mottled sky. All is heavy and damp. Moss and bracken and fleshy hart's-tongue ferns.

"A pony got stuck in the mire this morning," Sir Henry says. "I watched the poor thing struggle and die."

"A grim reality here," Dr. Mortimer says to me. "The bog is like quicksand in many places. There are islands of firm ground, but all the rest is ready to devour an unexpecting traveler."

I turn from the window, not wanting to think of the pony or the hungry mire. Instead, I move to further examine the wooden mannequin. The brass joints are of an intricate design, allowing for apparent rotation and extension. There's also a circular brass plate embedded in the center of the figure's chest with a phrase inscribed upon it in a language I believe to be Greek. The figure itself reminds me of an artist's model I once saw in the Hanover Gallery on New Bond Street. I made a remark to Holmes about what an uncanny thing the model was, so very alien in its appearance. Man and yet not man. And the Great Detective replied that there was nothing uncanny or alien about it, and I too often let my imagination get the best of me.

The mannequin's large ivory phallus is bizarrely engraved with a pastoral scene. Naked satyrs, horned and lithe, dance together in a forest around a fire. Each hooved figure has a curved erect phallus, a miniature of the mannequin's own. And the longer I study the engraving, the more it seems to me that the surrounding trees and the flames of the fire are erect. All the world, thick and veined and standing.

"If you could please remove the mannequin from my room," Sir Henry says. "Remove it and provide me with another dram of your elixir."

"You've already had your dram this morning," Dr. Mortimer says.

"Perhaps half a dram then?"

"I shall ask Barrymore to remove the mannequin. And I shall bring your second dram in an hour along with some hashed meat and biscuits."

Sir Henry sighs with relief. "That will be fine. Thank you. And it is good to meet you, Dr. Watson. I'm sorry to be in such a state. We can have a better conversation after I've rested."

"I look forward to it, Sir Henry," I reply.

"Barrymore has readied your quarters," Dr. Mortimer says after we've left Sir Henry's room and passed together down a dim and narrow hall. Our shadows trail along a wallpaper printed with charging wild boar.

"Doctor," I say. "The mannequin..."

"Ah, yes. Sir Henry suffers from what is referred to clinically as hysteria masculina. Are you familiar with the condition?"

Of course, I'd heard many stories of female hysterics—the wandering womb and all the trouble it causes—but I confess to knowing little about the male variety.

"The treatment I've devised is experimental," Dr. Mortimer says. "But very much in line with the general prescription—a consistent and thorough stimulation of the orifice."

"But with such an odd device?"

Dr. Mortimer dismisses my question with a wave of his hand. "Not so odd. Perhaps after you've gotten yourself settled, you'll join me in the natatorium. We can talk further about my research there."

"Natatorium?"

"A swimming pool. Modest but much appreciated.

Baskerville Hall comes fully equipped. You'll find a bathing suit in your room."

I nod, feeling unsure about all of this. "And the letter?"

Dr. Mortimer raises his well-groomed brow.

"You were about to show it to me in the parlor when Sir Henry called out."

"Oh yes," he says, patting his pockets. "I've honestly become so distracted in this house. I must have dropped it in my hurry on the stairs. I'll retrieve it now."

"What were its contents?"

"A threat in the form of a rather odd sketch. Occult in nature, I dare say. It's a drawing of the full moon with several lines slashed across its face. Sir Henry tells me the image represents a day and an hour. The Baskervilles have always possessed certain arcane knowledge, you understand."

"And what date was indicated?"

"The stroke of midnight. As Thursday turns to Friday this very week."

I pause. "We have only a few days then."

Dr. Mortimer nods. "If the interpretation is to be believed."

"I must report this to Holmes. He'll want to see the drawing. He learns much from such things."

"Of course," Dr. Mortimer says. "As soon as I locate it."

I am glad to see my room is near enough to Sir Henry's own that I will know if he's further disturbed. I intend to keep Dr. Mortimer's promise and do my very best to protect the young baronet.

I sit in the chair near my bed, bathing suit folded in my lap, considering my next action. I need to gather as much evidence as possible with the greatest amount of efficiency. And yet, as I attempt to formulate a plan, images of the mannequin impose themselves upon my rather bleary, travel-worn mind. The featureless face, the hard oaken body, the pale phallus rising. Holmes and I have come across many curious contraptions in our work together—the Mechanical Monk of St. Benedict's, Maelzel's Chess Player, the Golden Lions of the Caliphate—and yet nothing seems quite so curious to me as Dr. Mortimer's priapic device.

*There is also, of course, hysteria masculina. Upon returning to London, I must find my way to the medical library.*

*My return... impossible as it seems.*

*The cozy rooms at Baker Street: coat hooks and bearskin rug, velvet chairs and violin case, the little breakfast table, the bundles of manuscripts in every corner.*

*All these elements shift like the pieces of a puzzle box, trying to find a way to fit together again.*

*Now I cannot stop the rush of memories.*

*(Black ship upon a blacker sea... and the waves grow stronger still.)*

The mannequin and Sir Henry's relationship to it bring a grave deficiency to the forefront of my mind. Something that sets me apart from the many others I have met. An affliction that makes me lonelier too. I am able to forget sometimes. But as of late, there is no forgetting.

I think of Bernard, a country boy, and bunkmate of mine during my school days at Chelmsford. He was blond-haired and green-eyed. A spray of freckles across his delicate nose. Was I in love with him? Perhaps. Though my love has never mattered much.

"But John," he said one night as we held each other in his narrow bed, his stiffened cock pressed firmly against my thigh. "That's how everyone spends. We put ourselves inside one another's fundaments and move all about. It feels quite splendid."

"Well, it doesn't feel splendid to me," I said. "It's terribly painful. Like the turning of a knife."

He frowned. "You're not trying hard enough then."

"I am trying far harder than you can imagine."

"I don't believe you, John. And no one else is going to believe you either."

"Please," I said, reaching for his arm.

But before I could touch him, Bernard turned away.

And he did not turn back again.

*Holmes, too, of course. Great penetrator of the infinite mysteries.*

I wonder, for a moment, if I should speak with Dr. Mortimer about my deficiencies. My shame heaped upon years of shame. He would possibly be sympathetic to such a discussion due to his treatment of Sir Henry. And yet how could I be sure?

I remove the bottle of laudanum from my jacket pocket and take a long sip of sweet brown treacle. Opium settles upon me like a darkening sky... a faraway house... some final adventure.

When calmed, I don the striped bathing suit that fits as snuggly as a pair of long johns and wrap myself in a robe to make my way down the dim hall again. Sir Henry's room is silent, likely indicating the mannequin has been removed, and perhaps his dram has already been administered.

*How long did I sit in the chair beside my bed? How much time did I spend thinking of old Bernard and all the others?*

*I must remember to ask Dr. Mortimer what medicine he is administering to Sir Henry. I'll include it in the letter I send to Holmes by evening mail.*

I follow the winding stone staircase described by Dr. Mortimer into the cool lamplit depths of Baskerville Hall. And through a looming archway, I discover the natatorium, a most startling chamber indeed.

The room is long and narrow with a high vaulted ceiling. And the walls are painted with a vast mural, barely visible in the gaslight.

The mural shows aspects of an ancient city: broken towers, shattered domes, and empty boulevards. All sprawling beneath a red and starlit sky.

It strikes me almost immediately that this is supposed to be some depiction of Hell. Though why anyone would paint the underworld on the walls of a recreation room, I cannot begin to imagine.

I move toward the mural and realize that from behind the nearest pillar, some sort of hunched painted figure peers out at me. Its eyes are gold in color, shining in the half-light.

Due to the layers of shadow, I cannot discern whether it is a man or animal. Or maybe it has no proper form at all.

I think again of the Hound of the Baskervilles and the other supposed demons Sir Hugo raised from his pit. I wonder where that legendary crevasse might have been located. Was it inside Baskerville Hall?

I turn then toward the swimming pool itself, which is not, as Dr. Mortimer indicated, a modest affair. It is instead a most imposing structure, intricately tiled and painted with a flowering vine. Stained-glass lamps hang from the high ceiling, illuminating the water with a greenish glow.

As I step toward the pool, I realize I am not alone. A figure lounges at a low table in the far corner of the room. The table is in the shadow of a high oaken serving bar lined with bottles and glasses. I raise my hand in greeting, believing the figure must be Dr. Mortimer, but as I draw nearer, I realize it is a young woman. She wears a black bathing dress and a silk robe stitched with yellow chrysanthemums. Her face is powdery white. Her hair, dark and braided, is wound into a fashionable knot. She does not look, in any way, like a woman who belongs in the country.

"Dr. Watson?" she says, her voice cheerfully echoing through the chamber.

"Indeed."

"It's lovely to make your acquaintance. I've read so many of your little puzzles in The Strand. I'm Beryl Stapleton. My brother and I are staying at Merripit House on the moor."

I recognize the name of the house immediately. This is the woman Sir Henry called a witch, she who supposedly exalted the "powers of evil" and caused the death of a pony.

"Would you care to join me for a drink?" She gestures toward the bar. Her fingernails are painted a dark plum color, almost black.

"I'm waiting for Dr. Mortimer, I'm afraid. We are to continue a pressing conversation."

She smiles. "I'm sure he'll be around soon enough. And he'll likely enjoy a drink himself." She pats the chair beside her. "Please, come sit."

The swimming pool glows like a green cauldron. Bright spangles shift across the plains of the empty city.

"My brother is a naturalist with a keen interest in lepidoptery," Beryl Stapleton says. "When he's out catching his butterflies in the mire, I come here. Dr. Mortimer has invited us to swim whenever we like. And I have to admit it is a lovely respite from the cold and the damp. Don't you think so?"

"Quite," I say, for the natatorium is far warmer than the rest of the drafty house. There must be some sort of concealed heating element in the walls.

Beryl Stapleton rises and moves with a languid grace toward the serving bar. "I'm having what's called a Flash of Lightning," she says. "Brandy, gingerette, and a tablespoon of raspberry syrup. Shall I pour you one of those or something else?"

"A Flash of Lightening sounds delightful, Miss Stapleton."

She tips a decanter over a glass, splashing a dark liquid. "I've never met a man of letters before."

"No?"

"Or a detective."

"Oh, I assure you I am not a detective."

"Aren't you?" She sets the drink before me. It glistens in the light.

"I am merely an agent of Sherlock Holmes. And his biographer, I suppose."

"Or one might say his inventor," Beryl Stapleton replies.

"How's that?"

"Well, you must admit that, without you, Sherlock Holmes would exist as a man. But not as an idol."

"An interesting word."

She smiles vaguely. "You are a maker of gods, are you not, Dr. Watson?"

My cheeks grow warm with the heat of a blush. "I'm quite sure Holmes doesn't see it like that. He considers my accounts to be little more than childish ramblings that wreak havoc upon the truth of his actual exploits. I have, according to him, too Romantic an eye."

"How ungrateful," Beryl Stapleton says, taking a sip of her Flash of Lightening.

I follow suit and find the drink sweet and bright. Just the thing for a gloomy day. "This is very good," I say, taking another sip. And perhaps the alcohol emboldens me. "Since you're here, Miss Stapleton, I wonder if I might venture to ask you a few questions. We are investigating the death of Sir Charles Baskerville, as you are likely aware."

"Oh, poor Charlie, yes."

"You knew him?"

"He came to Merripit House on a few occasions to admire my brother's collections. Some artifacts of Neolithic man.

Skulls and hand axes. That sort of thing. You must come around yourself some time, Doctor. I'll give you a little tour."

"That sounds quite intriguing."

"A clan of ancient men used to inhabit the moor, you know. Their stone houses still remain. Imagine coming upon one of those strange old fellows prowling about. A heavy brow and blackish eyes, dragging some sort of awful mannish tool."

I draw my robe closer about my shoulders. "When was the last time you saw Sir Charles?"

"On the very day of his death," Beryl Stapleton says. "He was out walking. I was helping my brother search for the Cyclopides, a lovely velvet skipper moth. And we saw Charlie on the ridge and waved to him."

"Did you exchange any words?"

"He was too far in the distance and quite occupied."

"Oh?"

She nods. "Staring at the ground as if he'd lost something."

"Do you have any idea what he might have been looking for?"

"None at all. My brother said we must visit Sir Charles soon, and I agreed. But, of course, that was not to be."

"Do you know of any men who disliked him? Anyone who might have wanted to bring him harm?"

"I really wasn't apprised of his affairs. You'd be better off asking Lord V."

"Lord V?"

"A charmingly eccentric old man. Lord V of Laughter Hall. That's what he calls himself for reasons none of us quite understand. My brother and I had a very odd dinner there one evening. All sorts of theatrics. Smoke and mirrors. His house sits on the stony ridge above the moor, and he keeps a telescope on the roof. He sees everything from that vantage point. He may have even seen what happened to Charlie on the night of the murder, though he hasn't told anyone, of course. Generally, he's even more reclusive than the Baskervilles."

"I shall attempt to call upon him."

Beryl Stapleton runs a finger around the rim of her glass. "So you don't believe the rumors?"

"What rumors?"

"That an enormous spectral hound killed Charlie."

"I'm assuming all that is nothing more than the remains of some legend."

"Yes... I suppose." She pauses. "I find myself taking a rather keen interest in you, Dr. Watson. There are so few people to talk to on the moor. What if we were to play a little game together?"

"A game?"

"Something simple that might allow us to get to know each other better. For instance, I'll tell you one fact about myself if you tell me something about yourself. But it has to be true. Actually, it should be the truest thing you can think of."

I glance into Beryl Stapleton's dark eyes and wonder what exactly she might be driving at. Holmes would want me to engage in this game, as he seeks the truth at every turn, so I agree against my better judgment.

"Very good," she says. "You go first."

I look down into my drink. The truest thing...

That I am adrift?

That I am ingesting enough opium every day to fall a horse.

Or should I tell her the truth about Sherlock Holmes?

All the things I've never written. All that I would never write.

"You're thinking too much," she says. "The truest thing is often the first that leaps to mind."

I feel an even greater chill at this. "On second thought, Miss Stapleton, I don't believe I have time to play."

She looks disappointed. "I hope I didn't disturb you. I only meant—"

"I should really find Dr. Mortimer. And then I must make my way to Grimpen Village to post a letter by the evening mail."

"Well, maybe we'll try again one day."

"Perhaps." I stand, leaving half my drink. My legs feel unsure. I suppose the effects of the opium tincture mixed with the Flash of Lightning.

I move toward the stone arch and then turn back again.

Beryl Stapleton watches from her place at the low table.

There is an odd magnetism about her.

She floats in the dancing green light before the empty city. The plains of Hell.

"Good day," I say softly.

She raises a pale hand in return.

When I am halfway up the stairs, stumbling and staring at the ground, I encounter a large pair of leather boots and look up to see they are connected to the young servant, Barrymore.

He stands before me in all his dark-haired glory, holding a taper that illuminates the deliriously handsome surfaces of his faintly-bearded face.

I swim for an instant in his dark eyes. And the whole house seems to swim with me.

If I faint, Barrymore will catch me. I'll feel his arms, the tightly wound spring of his physique.

But I must not faint.

I must press on.

I place my hand upon the cool stone wall and gather my wits.

I mean to ask Barrymore if he knows the location of Dr. Mortimer, but before I can do so, he says in a hushed and hurried tone, "I would speak with you, sir."

My tongue feels too large for my mouth.

He casts a troubled glance behind him as if he believes someone might be close at his heels. "Please."

"But—what—" I say.

"Not here. I would speak in private. I am known of secrets."

"What secrets?"

He holds a finger to his lips (lips I wish I could kiss at that moment). "That which will interest you. Come to my room tonight, sir. After everyone has gone to bed. You'll find me at the back of the house near the Yew Alley. Pray, don't tell anyone."

"No," I say, still floating. "Of course not. No one at all."

# 3

Stumbling up from the natatorium, down a low and listing hall.

*Gas lamps hiss like serpents.*

I run my fingers over black wainscot and think of Barrymore. The handsome country fellow with all his strength about him. What has frightened him so?

*I know I must begin my letter to Holmes. I don't want to miss the evening mail. And yet...*

I find myself in a paneled gallery. Portraits of long-dead Baskervilles glare down at me. Men in lace-etched armor and broad plumed hats. Cragged landscapes and standing stones. Here is a woman in a forlorn parlor, eyes glinting, swaddled in a crush of damask. And here is a boy in white silk pajamas, clutching an albino ferret. Here, a spectral light. A parakeet. Stony towers. Rambling brooks. And then a vast flame-lit portrait with a brass plaque beneath: SIR HUGO BASKERVILLE. He who drew the Hound and the he-goat and the great lizard up from the pit. He wears the stiff red coat of a Royalist general, and his skin is the color of clotted cream.

Black hair falls in tendrilous curls. And his dark eyes seem to hold me, to study me, as if I myself am some devil drawn up from the nether realms. There's wickedness in his gaze, yes. But there is something else as well. A kind of desperate longing, perhaps? A will toward that which has not yet been seen?

In his one hand, Hugo Baskerville grips a broadsword. In the other, a book bound in some sort of yellow hide. There's a symbol embossed upon the book's cover: a full moon, dark craters like a hundred eyes.

I step toward the portrait, meaning to examine the pattern on the book.

"Evil thing, that," a male voice croaks behind me.

I nearly fall forward into the antique frame before turning to see the old groom who drove me in the wagonette from Grimpen Station. He must be some eighty years of age, standing stooped and palsied, craning his neck to gaze up at the portrait.

"That is Sir Hugo's devil book," he says.

I place my hand on the wall to steady myself. "Is it?"

"My wife discovered it in the house some years ago during the time of Rodger Baskerville. She opened the wretched thing, for the poor woman had a curious mind and nearly fainted because of what she read there."

"What exactly did she read?"

"His lordship's vicious writings. Accounts of his exploits and his incantations."

I can see now how bloodshot the old groom's eyes are, and so too his nose and cheeks. Likely flushed from years of drink. "Incantations?" I say.

He nods feebly. "That which he used to control nature."

"And where is the book now?"

The old man shakes his head. "Gone away. As so many things are. Today is not like yesterday."

"No. It's certainly not."

He peers at me. "You do not look well, sir."

I put a hand to my forehead and find I am damp with sweat. I wonder about Beryl Stapleton's Flash of Lightening. Was it possible she put something in my drink? What reason would she have for taking such an action, though? "I think I need to rest," I say.

"You should find your rest then, sir. Baskerville Hall does not sit well with all men."

I glance toward the dark corridor beyond the gallery. "Do you know where I might find Dr. Mortimer?"

"Oh, I saw the doctor walking on the moorland road. That man walks for miles despite his limp. He won't be back till evening time."

I lower my head.

"Do you need assistance?"

The idea of asking for assistance from one so feeble seems ridiculous, even in my current state. "I'll find my own way."

He makes a little bow. "I am Perkins the groom. Call upon me if you should have the need."

"Thank you, Perkins. I'll do that."

*The house is even larger than I first understood. Crumbling old wings. So many rambling halls. In some places, the ceiling has fallen in, and light from a dead sky shines through. Doves flutter in the rafters. Blackish vines threaten to overtake the whole of it.*

*

After some searching, I finally locate my room. I mean to sit at the writing desk and pen my letter to Holmes, but as soon as I see my bed, I fall face-first into it. I awake later with a start, unsure where I am, believing at first I'm back at Baker Street, and Holmes stands in the doorway, a tall silhouette. Focus your attentions, Watson. Now is not the time for foolishness.

> *The sun has passed its zenith. I dash off the letter to Holmes, enumerating the facts I've gathered and imploring him to come at once. I explain the symbol Dr. Mortimer described: the full moon with slashes across its face. (And why is there a second moon on Hugo Baskerville's so-called devil book?) The moon means Thursday, midnight, Holmes. If Sir Henry doesn't surrender the house by then, he believes he will suffer the same fate as his cousin. We must bring this case swiftly to a close.*

I hurry down to the stables, thinking I will ask Perkins the groom to drive me to Grimpen Village in the wagonette. Holmes warned I must personally deliver all of my messages to the postmaster. "We cannot allow our opponent's eyes to happen upon your words, Watson, whoever that opponent may be. When the game is afoot, we must always be sure to keep the upper hand." But I find no one in the stable. There is only an open Bible and an empty wine cup. Perkins too, is gone away, it would seem.

*

Grimpen Village is no more than four miles across the moor. And I decide a brisk walk would do me good. I'll keep to the moorland road so as not to get stuck in the hungry mire and suffer the fate of the pony.

I set out along a gray and lonely path.

*Jagged sinister hills break the gloomy curve of the brackish moor.*
*There's a cold wind. A scent of damp heather.*

The nearly full moon takes its place in the evening sky above a circle of standing stones, a megalith likely erected by the Neolithic hunters Beryl Stapleton described. At the center of the circle is some kind of carved granite altar. I wonder what sort of sacrifices might have once been performed in this place.

*Two ravens land before me on the quiet path.*
*Yellow leaves fall.*

Grimpen village is a gathering of old dark houses and cramped cobbled streets. Doors are firmly shut. Smoke billows from chimneys. A black tavern looms before the village green. Someone has carved faces into turnips and beets and placed them in the tavern's windows. The vegetables grin at me through the rippled glass. I recognize this ritual as a means of warding off evil spirits. And I wonder what sort of bogies the villagers might fear.

I find the postmaster, a sallow bespectacled man of forty, in a lamplit shop and give him my letter addressed to Baker Street. I ask if I've missed the evening mail, and he assures me I have not. Holmes will have my letter soon enough. Perhaps he'll send a reply by tomorrow afternoon.

Before I depart, the postmaster hands me a printed flyer:

*GRIMPEN HARVEST FAIR*
*THURSDAY, OCTOBER 16th*
*NOONTIDE*

At the bottom of the flyer, a skeleton rests beneath a leafless tree.

I thank the postmaster and say I'll certainly return for the fair if time permits.

I am feeling more myself as I make my way back along the moorland road. The moon has risen higher in a violet sky. I sing one of my old soldiering songs to keep myself company. Where are the boys of the old brigade who fought with us side by side? Shoulder to shoulder and blade by blade, fought till they fell and died.

I pause to look once more at the megalith, the circle of Neolithic stones, and the granite altar enclosed within. And as I stand there on the lonely road, something remarkable occurs. Two tall women in simple linen dresses walk up out of the brush and pass over the path. At first, I think my eyes deceive me, for the pair are almost wraithlike. They make no sound. Their bodies do not even seem to disturb the air. It's as if I'm looking at a misty daguerreotype. But this is a daguerreotype that moves. Their long auburn tresses are woven with bog flowers. Gorse and purple heather. Oxeye daisy. They do not glance at me or even seem to notice I am watching. Instead, they walk with purpose toward the circle of standing stones and pass between two of the largest blocks. Then the women do not appear again.

I shift my position on the road, trying to spot them. But the circle is empty. The altar stands alone.

Two shirtless men appear a few minutes later, beautiful in their old-fashioned leather breeches. Their hair is long and windblown. And the bones of their faces are broad and strong like the bones of warriors. They, too, pay me no mind as they pass over the road, and soon they disappear between the largest of the standing stones as well.

I want to call out, but there is something so strange about these occurrences, as if they are not actually happening at all.

I think of a description of fairies I once encountered in an old spiritualist's manual. The book claimed such creatures are the ancient dead. Ancestors transformed into something like gods.

But I do not believe in fairies, of course. Or gods, for that matter.

*I will ask Dr. Mortimer what might bring young men and women onto the moor in the evening time. Perhaps they are practicing some pageant for the harvest fair?*

As I turn to leave, a sound stops me. A long low cry. Indescribably sad.

It fills the whole of the air, rising to a kind of wail.

And it seems to crash over me like a wave in some invisible inland sea.

The wave makes me terribly cold and causes me to think not only of what might be out there on the moor but also of my own heart.

The despair that weighs upon me.

The sound comes again. I hope it might be the call of some bird. And yet it is nothing like a bird. It sounds like—

I think of Beryl Stapleton, sipping her Flash of Lightning: "So you don't believe the rumors... that an enormous spectral hound killed Charlie?"

Another cry, wilder still.

And is it closer too?

I take my pistol from my coat pocket and hurry along the darkening road back to Baskerville Hall, glancing behind me every so often to ensure I am not followed.

Dr. Mortimer remains in absence. No one seems to be about, in fact. So I return to my room and lock the door, trying to forget the wailing sound. I take two sips of laudanum, and when I am finally calmed, I fall into a half-sleep.

*My dreams: A black dog. Barrymore, dark-eyed and virile in the moonlight. Skeletons of men and animals crawling from the carnivorous bog.*

I wake to a new sound. Someone walks in the hall beyond my room. A heavy dragging step. The interloper pauses just outside my door as if listening for something and then moves on. I do not want to open the door and encounter whatever figure lurks there. I refuse to invite another mystery. Instead, I close my eyes and will myself to fall asleep again.

When I awake a second time, I check my pocket watch. It's nearly ten p.m. The house is silent, and I am famished. I realize I have not eaten all day, and I determine I must find the kitchen before my late-night interview with Barrymore. I grow momentarily excited at the prospect of visiting his room alone. But then I promptly tell myself to stop acting like a fool. Nothing will happen between the two of us. Country fellows are not interested in such dalliances. I return instead to my thoughts of food. For supper is at least a possibility. Surely there must be a cook at Baskerville Hall.

I get out of bed and crack the door, gazing down the threadbare runner toward the flickering gas lamp. The hall is empty except for the bristled boar running through the wallpaper. Whoever walked with a dragging step is gone.

I exit my bedroom and pass the closed door of Sir Henry's silent bedchamber before descending the oaken stair. I hope the baronet is resting well.

I explore a maze of rooms, finally discovering a grand dining room hung with black damask. Candelabras stand unlit on a long, polished table. A paneled door hidden in the wall leads to a white-tiled kitchen where I find an icebox. Thankfully, the remains of a leftover hen have been stored inside.

As I sit picking at the hen, I think of Dr. Mortimer. He seems to have purposefully abandoned me, and I wonder what that might mean. He was so intent upon having Holmes and me come to the house, so urgent in his descriptions of the strange goings-on. And yet now he is suddenly absent, having not even provided me with the letter he promised.

I exit the dining room and hear a faint moan from the upper floors. I believe I recognize the voice as that of Sir Henry, and I hurry up the stairs to check on him, for there is apparently no one else who might come to his aid.

I stand before Sir Henry's door and listen. The moaning indeed comes from inside the room, and there is some other noise, too, a low and rhythmic creaking. I tap lightly on the door. Receiving no answer, I tap louder still.

The moaning intensifies, and I convince myself it's likely an utterance of sorrow or pain. I grasp the brass knob and turn it, opening the door a crack to peer inside. What I see is as startling to me as anything I could imagine.

Sir Henry lies supine and naked on a coil of sheets surrounded by silken pillows. His finely made legs are spread. His long thin cock, swollen. On top of him is the wooden mannequin, the invention of Dr. Mortimer. The tip of the mannequin's tusk-like phallus is inserted into Sir Henry's fundament, and the figure is slowly and mechanically penetrating the baronet. With each of the mannequin's creaking thrusts, Sir Henry emits another long low moan and clutches fiercely at the pillows. At one point, the baronet lifts his arms and puts them around the mannequin's wooden back, scaping at the lacquer there with his fingernails.

The mannequin continues its thrusts, moving ever deeper. When the carved phallus is buried almost to its hilt inside Sir Henry, the baronet lets out a final cry and a thick jet of ejaculate issues from his cock.

I must make some sound myself for, very slowly and in tandem, Sir Henry and the mannequin turn their heads to look at me.

Sir Henry's face is blank, sweat-damp hair plastered to his brow. His dark eyes look, but they do not see. Clearly, he's lost in some drug-addled haze.

The mannequin, of course, has no face whatsoever. Yet somehow, it regards me. I feel observed, deeply so, by its flat wooden visage.

Silently, I close the door, praying the baronet will not call out.

I lower myself to the hall floor.

This house... I do not know what to make of it.

With a shaking hand, I reach for the bottle of laudanum.

# 4

*The baronet's moaning has mercifully ceased, and I have crept back to my chambers. My hand trembles as I make these notes. For what exactly did I see?*

*Clockwork horror.*

*Wood and brass and ivory.*

*Has the mannequin returned to sit limply in its cane back chair once more? Will the same infernal scene play out again tomorrow?*

*I need only record facts, of course. Holmes will sort all of this out later. Except one of the facts in this instance is so outlandish, I can barely write it, no less believe it is true. For the mannequin actually turned its head to look at me. As if it was aware of my presence. Somehow more aware than Henry Baskerville himself.*

*Sir Henry's eyes (like burned-out bulbs).*

*Sir Henry's jaw (a loosened hinge).*

*I remember a theory of the ancient Greeks presented in one of my medical texts: Pneuma, a vital air that animates the body. And there was some discussion too (in the writings of Hippocrates, perhaps?) of isolating that air to animate the inanimate. Nonsense, of course. And yet what exactly has Dr. Mortimer done here to enact his so-called cure?*

*It's nearly midnight. I must somehow compose myself. My time with Barrymore is close at hand.*

*I remove my shoes so I can walk quietly.*

*I do not want to rouse Sir Henry. And I certainly do not want to draw the attention of the mannequin.*

*Every creak of the oaken stair excites my nerves.*

*I make my way down the long central hall to the back of the silent manor, where leaded glass doors lead out onto the Yew Alley. The alley itself is a gloom-ridden tunnel of trees half-lit by the ivory glow of the moon. This is where Charles Baskerville met his end. And I realize I have yet to inspect the crime scene. Holmes would berate me, of course. But there is no time to step into the Yew Alley now. Barrymore is waiting.*

I find the dour servant's hall all but abandoned. A single crack of light streams from beneath the left's final door. "Barrymore," I whisper, almost inaudibly. Despite the tentative nature of my call, the door creaks open to reveal the young man himself. He's still dressed in his dark woolen trousers and white butler's shirt with the turned-up collar. But now, two of the shirt's buttons are undone, revealing a fine pale chest beneath. There's a palpable strength in Barrymore's presence, yet his dark eyes are wide and fearful as he beckons me into his room.

After I am safely inside, he closes the door and bolts it.

I notice the scent first, that of a young man living alone. An acrid smell, but something sweeter too. Like an extract of vanilla. I feel intoxicated and will myself not to become dizzy. I must attend to the task at hand.

Barrymore's chamber is a humble one: a small bed, a wooden chair, and a low shelf holding two picture books. One of the books demonstrates physical exercises for athletes, and the other is called London for a Day: Scenes of the City. A taper, the only source of light in the room, burns beside a tin cup and a basin for water.

"I do apologize for hurrying you in, sir," Barrymore says in a quiet voice. "My nerves, they are all ajangle." He rubs one hand over his bearded jaw. "When I first heard your step, I thought it might be—" He trails off.

"You thought it might be who?"

"Him who roams the manor, sir."

"Him?"

"I do not know his face. I have not dared look upon it."

"You must take a breath," I say. "There's no one roaming about this evening but me."

"I only hope that might be true." He gestures toward the wooden chair. "Do you care to sit? I'm sorry there's not more comfort here."

I take a seat, and Barrymore sits on the bunk opposite. The room is so small our knees nearly touch. And the crisply made bed reminds me of my days in the Fifth Northumberland. The camaraderie of cheerful men. There was a particularly boisterous soldier, a sharpshooter named Ephraim, who had a most rakish smile. I tried to kiss him once behind a tent in Candahar after we'd shared a bottle of Scotch whisky. And though he declined my advance, he was kind. He said he did not care for men in such a way. But he did care for me. "As brothers, John."

I lean forward. "Tell me what you mean to say, Barrymore."

"It's all fine and well during the light of day," he says. "But at night, that's when he comes."

"Who comes? You must be clear if I'm to help you."

He looks at me carefully, and I hope I do not appear too haggard in his eyes. "You are a detective, aren't you? That's what I've heard."

"I'm a physician by trade. But I work with a detective, yes."

"A friend of mine in the village used to tell me stories. All sorts of things about crimes and such. And when I did my chores, I'd pretend this house was full of what is called 'clues.' But I realized there's nothing like clues here. It's all just such a desperate mess."

"We'll try to make sense of it tonight. I promise you. But you must explain in some detail first."

He lifts the tin cup from the shelf and offers it to me. "Do you want to drink some water, sir?"

"No. Thank you, though."

He takes a healthy drink himself, and I try not to stare too longingly at the bobbing of his Adam's apple. "It started before the death of his lordship, Sir Charles," he says, wiping water from his lips with the back of his hand. "Several months before. I would wake in the night and hear someone moving about. I knew it could not be Sir Charles or Sir Henry, for they both slept quite soundly due to the medicine Dr. Mortimer administers. Then I thought it might be Dr. Mortimer himself, for he walks with a limp, and whatever moved about in the halls also seemed to drag its foot. But even when the doctor was gone, I heard the odd, furtive step. I knew it could not be Perkins, for he sleeps in rooms behind the stables and does not enter the house at night. So there is no one else, you see. No one at all."

"I believe I heard just such a sound earlier," I say, remembering my half-waking state. "Someone moved down the hall with a dragging step."

"You heard him then." Barrymore glances at the door, perhaps to make sure it's still securely bolted. "He comes and goes as he pleases. Sometimes he disappears for days. But he always returns. He's looking for something. And I worry... I worry he might be looking for me."

"Why you?"

He shakes his head. "I don't know, sir. Honestly, I don't."

"Well, you mustn't let this get the best of you. There's an answer to every puzzle. A most logical one. I've learned that from my years of working with Sherlock Holmes."

"Mr. Holmes, yes." Barrymore places the tin cup carefully back on the shelf.

"You told me earlier you know some secret. Was this what you were talking about? That someone stalks the halls at night?"

"It was not, sir."

I raise my brow. "What is the secret then?"

"I cannot explain in words. I must show you." He stands. "We have to be quiet, though. I don't want him who walks to hear us."

I take the pistol from my coat pocket and show it to Barrymore.

He makes a low whistling sound. "I've never heard of a doctor who carries a gun."

"Well, my boy," I reply. "I suppose you must assume I am an uncommon sort of doctor."

Barrymore takes the burning taper from his shelf and leads

me into the hall. We pass along a series of darkened corridors and finally arrive at the stone staircase where I encountered him earlier in the day. We descend and enter the vault of the natatorium that's now black as pitch. The only light comes from the taper, and I must remain close at Barrymore's side so as not to stumble. He smells faintly of Bergamot, the scent of some rural tonic perhaps. And as our footsteps echo in the darkness, I will myself not to lean even closer to him.

Barrymore guides me to the section of the painted mural I noted earlier, where some sort of hunched figure with golden eyes lurks behind a broken pillar.

"I discovered this while cleaning one morning," he says.

"I noticed it as well. An odd image."

"Not the picture, sir." He holds his taper near the mural. "Look here."

The candle flame reveals a seam running along the wall that forms the outline of a door. Barrymore presses a spot on the creature's forehead just above its golden eyes, and the panel releases, swinging open to reveal a dark stone tunnel.

"I must admit this house is full of surprises," I say.

He moves down the passage, and I follow, glancing back every so often into the darkness.

We walk for what feels like ten minutes, finally arriving at a second stone staircase, this one carved into the earth itself.

"Deeper still, is it?" I ask.

"Ever deeper, I'm afraid," Barrymore replies.

We descend and come to the entrance of a limestone cavern. There's a sound of running water and a faint smell of sulfur. Inside the cave, astonishingly, is a narrow underground river flowing gently in the darkness. I have heard of England's lost rivers, of course. The Fleet and the Tyburn are said to move beneath London itself. But I have never seen such a thing. Nor even dreamed I would.

The light from Barrymore's taper reveals a small flatbottom boat tethered at the water's edge. He steps into the boat and uses a long oar to steady the craft as he helps me inside. After I'm seated, he unfastens the moorings, and we float down the dark stream through a narrow tunnel. I hold the taper while Barrymore steers. The walls of the cave are damp, covered in glistening algae.

As we round the bend, I catch sight of movement on the wall above. A small, nearly-translucent creature scuttles between two outcroppings. It's composed of what appears to be a toad's bulbous head and a serpent's body. But unlike a serpent, it uses a pair of thin jointed legs to propel itself.

The creature watches us with yellow lamp-like eyes. And when we are very close, it scuttles off into the darkness.

"What was that?" I ask. "Some breed of salamander?"

"There are all sorts of animals down here, sir," Barrymore replies in an oddly flat tone. "They are not like other animals I have seen."

"No," I say. "Not like other animals at all."

The boat rocks uneasily in the black river. Soon we encounter what looks to be some sort of albino bat. It uses hooked fingers to crawl along the ceiling, white fur wet and matted. When the bat raises its head, I realize that it has a long sharp beak full of jagged teeth instead of a rodent-like muzzle. Its black eyes reflect the light of the taper.

"They're not dangerous? These creatures?"

"No, sir," Barrymore replies. "They are in a state of confusion. There's something down here that occupies them. A tremor in the earth. You'll feel it soon enough."

We round another bend, and a weird long-legged shape steps forward and stands in the shadows of the river. It reminds me of a stork or heron in the way it moves. But it has a wizened, almost intelligent face. Something that looks nearly human.

"My God," I say, for I can barely comprehend what I'm looking at.

"Only the smaller animals come through on their own," Barrymore says. "They get lost up here in the dark."

"There are larger animals too?"

"Yes," he says. "But someone has to help the larger ones through."

Barrymore tethers the boat at a second dock that's covered in yellow fungi and takes the taper from me. I worry that the flame will eventually burn out if we are down here too long. We'll be stranded in the black cave with the eerie watchful creatures. But surely Barrymore must know what he's doing. Surely, he must.

Another tunnel opens before us, and around its entrance, someone has painted arcane symbols, all in white. I recognize a rendering of the many-eyed moon as I follow Barrymore inside. Unseen bodies scuttle and scratch at the walls. Something chitters at us from above.

There is a feeling here like the pull of some magnet. But I am not only pulled by it. The sensation surrounds me. Pressed on all sides.

And there's a sound too. A hush or a hiss. Soft at first. Growing louder. And the louder the sound becomes, the more I begin to believe it is not an external noise but something inside my own head.

I wish I could take Barrymore's hand. I want to find comfort in his presence. But I resist such an urge, for I do not know what the boy's reaction might be.

Soon we arrive at a wide stone chamber. On the floor of the chamber is something difficult to see. It appears, at first, to be a long narrow shadow. But that's impossible, of course, for there is no source of light other than our candle's flame. As we approach, I realize it is not a shadow at all. It's a black fissure. A crevasse leading deep into the earth. The odd sound that seems to come from inside my head is much louder here. A river rushing through my skull.

"I believe this to be the pit from the old legend, sir," Barrymore says.

"Legend?"

"The one Dr. Mortimer told you about when you arrived. This is Sir Hugo's pit. Where he performed his rituals."

I look again at the fissure before us and understand Barrymore's meaning. He thinks this hole is the mythic chasm from which Hugo Baskerville drew his impossible demons: the lizard, the he-goat, and the great Hound. But all of that is certainly nothing more than a lurid old tale.

Barrymore approaches the fissure's edge and rests his taper against a stone. The flickering light reveals the bodies of small pale animals surrounding the rim of the pit, clinging to its cragged sides. Some of the animals are like fish with the legs of centipedes. Others are like large white beetles or tendrilled mollusks. There's a soft, gelatinous mass with no features except for a dark spot at its center that may or may not be a watchful eye.

The sound is deafening now. A roaring hush.

Barrymore turns toward me. In these shadows, he looks even more beautiful. A faun cut from the lines of some dark pastoral. "It makes me feel so odd, sir," he says.

I reach out to comfort him, to finally touch him. My fingers tremble.

Barrymore takes my hand and pulls me toward the fissure. "Come look what's inside. It's what I wanted to show you."

I find reaching the pit's edge difficult, for the sound is like a mire. It drags at my arms and legs.

When we finally arrive at the rim, we look down into a shifting darkness that is almost flesh-like in nature. A series of sliding soft surfaces. Hazy. Unformed. As if new parts of the world move beneath us. There is a light somewhere in the fissure too. Pulsing and rose-colored. Far away. A light that seems to exist beyond the spectrum of the human eye.

I gaze into the crevasse. And Barrymore gazes too.

I do not remember when I turned toward him or when he turned toward me. But soon we face each other. And some part of me realizes we are no longer exactly like ourselves. We are more like the sound that comes from the fissure. The roaring hush. An empty thing. And we are like the sliding shadows in the pit as well. We pull at each other. Softly at first. Then with greater strength. As if we have been in some argument and mean to topple one another.

Briefly, I wonder if some kind of toxin rises from the pit.

Perhaps we are affected by poisonous gas.

But before I can speak this fear out loud, my thoughts are covered over by the hushing sound. I am submerged.

Barrymore and I struggle there upon the rim. I am pressed to him, as I have been pressed to so many men. His body tenses. And the whole world trembles. Every atom. We kneel together at the edge of the pit amongst the weird animals as if we meant to pray.

Our actions grow increasingly obscure, performed as if within the circle of a dream. Soon we lie naked on the ground. Barrymore, pale and hard. And I, a softer thing.

For a moment, he is not Barrymore at all. He is Sherlock Holmes. Not the man I wrote about for so many years, but the man himself. He is all the nights Holmes and I spent together in the same bed. Sometimes holding each other. But more often turned away, facing our respective walls, wandering the corridors of private thoughts.

And yet Barrymore is not like Holmes, for he does not turn away. He looks at me with dark, handsome eyes. I press my stiff cock against his. I kiss his throat, his chest, tasting the salt of him. I move my mouth down his body until I arrive at the swollen head of his prick. And he is in my mouth. Sliding in and out between my lips, growing ever stiffer. Ever more full.

We move together, throbbing like the rose-colored light,

hushing like the sound. And finally, he bursts. Flooding my throat.

I swallow him. I drink him down. The pit roars behind us. And the taper's flame is suddenly doused.

## 5

*How long do I sleep there in the cave beside the fissure?*

*I cannot say with any certainty.*

*I only know that I awake to a watery light streaming down from the vault's cragged ceiling.*

*The fissure itself has quieted. The trembling is now nothing more than a distant rumble.*

*And I feel almost like myself again, or at least a weary, pained semblance of that self.*

*Memories flutter in the dark. Recollections of the night before.*

I lift my head to see Barrymore is no longer beside me in the cavern. I call out for him once and then again. There's no response. And I numbly wonder why he has left me all alone.

This question goes unanswered.

But at least there is the light. It emanates from a high corner of the chamber. And as it intensifies, a miracle is revealed—a staircase, previously concealed in shadow.

The stairs are carved from stone, descending from the dark roof of the cave.

I gather my clothes piece by piece and ascend, emerging into a cold gray morning.

I realize almost immediately where I find myself. The Neolithic stones stand like guardians in a circle around me.

I am inside the megalith upon the moor. I've come through some trapdoor near the granite altar. The door itself is shaped like an ancient wheel, and someone has rolled it aside. Was it Barrymore? I put on my clothes, all the while thinking of him. The two of us together in the earth. I wonder if he was frightened by what happened. Or perhaps repelled. Is that why he left me there by the crevasse?

Morning birds scream overhead as I slowly make my way back to Baskerville Hall.

Perkins the old groom, struggles to carry a bushel of hay across the stable yard and pauses to watch my approach. "Are you faring better, sir?" he calls in his rasping voice.

I realize there can be no answer to such a question, so I merely nod and raise my hand.

"That is well and good," he replies. "Well and good."

When I enter the house, I am greeted by the scent of side meat and the clinking of dishes.

"Dr. Watson?" a male voice calls out. "Is that you?"

I move slowly toward the sound, realizing just how much my bones ache with every step. I am far too old to spend the night on the hard stone floor of a cavern.

Dr. Mortimer sits in a brightly lit breakfast parlor with a napkin tucked in his shirtfront. Before him are an array of gold-trimmed dishes piled with everything from rashers to pickled herring to marmalade. He sips at a steaming cup of tea. "I've been looking everywhere for you," he says, taking note of the rumpled condition of my clothes. "Were you out walking?"

I am unsure how much I should reveal to Dr. Mortimer. Barrymore asked me not to tell anyone about our meeting. Who exactly can be trusted in this house?

"I've been out, yes."

Dr. Mortimer must hear the strain in my voice, for he stands and moves toward me. "Please, sit. Let me pour you some tea."

I do as he asks, for the tea smells strong and good.

"Cream?" Dr. Mortimer asks.

I shake my head and take the steaming cup with trembling hands.

"Are you sure you're quite all right, Dr. Watson?"

"I am... unsure," I say. For that is the truth. I feel the cave inside me. And I see the fissure too. The great crack in the earth that leads to—but where might such a passage lead?

"Dear me," Dr. Mortimer says. "Here, let me serve you some herring."

He fills my plate, and I stare down at the rather greasy-looking fish, thinking of the pale many-legged bodies in the cave.

I want to ask the whereabouts of Barrymore, but I hold my tongue. Instead, I say, "Why did you leave the house yesterday?"

"I was called away on an emergency visit," Dr. Mortimer replies. "I still treat a portion of the county, you understand. This was a case of pleurisy. Rather severe. Then, because the hour was so late, I returned to my own house in Postbridge and spent the night." He takes a bite of toast and chews thoughtfully. "Now, I've come to check on Sir Henry and to speak with you about what I think we must do next."

"The letter," I say. I want to ask instead about the priapic mannequin in Sir Henry's room. And about what Dr. Mortimer has done to create such an impossible machine. But that discussion must wait. I cannot bear further strangeness now.

"Oh yes, of course," he says, taking a piece of parchment from his pocket and laying it before me on the table. A charcoal sketch of the full moon (the many-eyed moon) stares back at me. A dark red slash runs horizontally across the moon's face, and another runs diagonally. The image means nothing to me. And there is no further information apparent. Holmes will likely see something, though. A watermark. A stray hair. A thumbprint.

"There is a detail I didn't have time to tell you yesterday," Dr. Mortimer says. "A theory that may or may not be of significance."

"Go on."

"Whoever is behind all this might be engaged in some sort of plot laid out by the bringer of the curse himself."

"Hugo Baskerville?"

Dr. Mortimer nods.

"But he is long dead."

"Yes, though he kept a careful record of his intentions in—"

"A book bound in a yellow hide," I say.

Dr. Mortimer raises his brow. "I thought it was Sherlock Holmes who was supposed to shock us with his foreknowledge, Dr. Watson."

"Hugo Baskerville holds the book in the portrait gallery."

"Oh yes," Dr. Mortimer says. "The book with a moon embossed on its cover. Very like the moon in the letter, don't you think?"

I gaze down at the sketch, considering its many eyes.

"At any rate, it is possible that if we discover who is in possession of the book, we will have found our murderer."

"Where does this theory come from?"

Dr. Mortimer pauses as if unsure whether to reveal his source. "Beryl Stapleton," he says finally.

"What would she know about all of this?"

"You likely heard Sir Henry refer to her as a witch yesterday. And though I don't think that's true, she does possess a great deal of esoteric knowledge. I've had a number of useful conversations with her and—"

"And you've invited her to come and go in this house as she pleases."

"How do you know that?"

"I met her in the natatorium yesterday when I was supposed to meet with you. She didn't mention anything about the book."

"Well," Dr. Mortimer says. "I'm not sure how much she trusts this investigation."

"Why should she not?"

"It's a delicate matter. Do you know when Sherlock Holmes is arriving?"

"I should have word today. I expect him to—"

A voice from somewhere at the back of the house suddenly interrupts us. "Dead! Oh, he is dead!"

Dr. Mortimer stands abruptly, knocking over his cup of tea. A dark stain spreads across the tablecloth. "Dead?" he says. And then, under his breath: "Please say it's not Sir Henry."

The voice calls out again, "Dead, I say! Dead!"

I follow Dr. Mortimer toward the back of the house, and when we arrive at the leaded glass doors of the Yew Alley, I see Perkins, the old groom, standing unsteadily over a dark shape outside.

Dr. Mortimer flings open the double doors, revealing that Perkins stares down at the lifeless body of a man. A large stone has been dropped on the man's head, crushing it. The stone remains in place, streaked with gore, entirely obscuring the face.

But the clothing, the dark trousers and white shirt with the turned-up color, I recognize this uniform immediately. And I feel as though my heart is falling. Crashing through a thousand false floors.

"Dear God," Dr. Mortimer says, kneeling beside the body. "It's Barrymore."

# 6

I fall to my knees before the body.

How can it be that Barrymore's handsome face is crushed beneath this bloodied stone?

I clutch at his waist. I cannot speak.

The poor boy told me he feared an intruder who walked the halls at night, a man with a dragging step. He said this man was menacing him. And what did I do in response? I waived my pistol about. As if such a meager weapon could protect any of us held here in the terrible sway of Baskerville Hall.

I choke back a sob, not caring if Dr. Mortimer or Perkins observes, for what does anything matter if such horrors as this are permitted?

Then from the leaded glass doors, a woman's voice: "Dear God, who is that?"

I turn, and through my tears, I see Beryl Stapleton, coifed and manicured, emerging into the Yew Alley. She wears a dark silk robe covered in crescent moons over a bathing suit and carries a steaming cup of morning tea.

"Miss Stapleton," Dr. Mortimer says. "Perhaps you should go back inside. This is a rather gruesome business, I'm afraid."

"Don't mollycoddle me, Doctor," She takes a step closer to Barrymore's body. "I came up from the natatorium because

I heard all the commotion. Now do tell me who is under that rock."

"It's Barrymore," Dr. Mortimer says.

"The servant boy?"

He nods grimly.

"And what are you doing on top of him, Dr. Watson?" she asks.

I clear my throat and attempt a response. But instead of words, I utter a brief, strangled cry.

"Dr. Watson has not been feeling himself these last days," Perkins intones.

"Two doctors," Beryl Stapleton says, "and the carriage driver makes a diagnosis."

"Please, Miss Stapleton," Dr. Mortimer says. "If you'll just step inside. We'll—"

"I admit this is terrible," Beryl Stapleton says. "But that is most certainly not the servant boy. I just passed him in the hall. He's carrying linens, looking slightly muddled as usual. But very much alive.

"What?" I say. "Barrymore is alive?"

"You can crawl down off of whoever that is, Doctor," Beryl Stapleton says.

I look at the body again. Several buttons on the blood-spattered shirt are undone. The corpse's chest, I realize, is covered in curly brown hair. And his shoulders and waist are of a much denser nature than Barrymore's own.

"Boy?" Beryl Stapleton calls into the house. "Are you in there? Come show yourself."

Soon enough, Barrymore emerges from the shadows.

He wears a white shirt and a pair of dark woolen trousers identical to those of the corpse. When he sees the body, he blanches and recoils.

"Barrymore!" I say, overjoyed.

He looks at me in fear.

"Can you explain why this man appears to be wearing your clothes?" Dr. Mortimer says.

But before Barrymore can respond, another voice issue from inside the house, this one male is rather hysterical. "What is happening here?" Henry Baskerville emerges into the Yew Alley wearing a nightshirt. His hair is wildly tousled, and he looks as though he hasn't slept for days.

He peers down at the body and presses a hand to his mouth.

"Sir Henry," Dr. Mortimer says, stepping in front of the baronet to block his view of the corpse. "You must return to your bed."

"My cousin," Sir Henry gasps. "My beloved Charles."

"It's not Charles, my lord," Dr. Mortimer says. "Charles is in the churchyard. You know that very well."

"I'm going to die here, aren't I?" Henry Baskerville says. "On Thursday when the clock chimes midnight."

"No. You're under our protection."

"Who is this man?" he asks. "How could such a thing have happened again?"

Beryl Stapleton takes a sip of tea. "I suppose that's exactly what we're trying to determine, isn't it?"

"You!" Henry Baskerville says, pointing a thin white finger at her.

"Me?" she says.

"Who let her into my house?" He regards all of us with an accusatory gaze.

"Clearly, I let myself in," she replies. "The devil is very good about unlocking doors when you say the right prayers."

"Witch," Sir Henry says.

"You've never had much of a sense of humor, have you, Henry?"

"Leave this house! Do not return."

Beryl Stapleton sighs and nods to Dr. Mortimer and me. "I'll talk to you gentlemen later, I suppose." With that, she hands Henry Baskerville her half-full cup of tea and exits through the leaded glass doors.

Sir Henry stares down at the teacup as if it is a figuration of evil.

"May I take that from you, sir?" Perkins says, stepping forward with an unsteady gait.

Sir Henry returns his attention to the corpse. "Is anyone going to lift that stone from atop his head?"

"What's underneath will be quite unpleasant," Dr. Mortimer replies. "And we should wait for the constable so as not to disturb the evidence."

The baronet closes his eyes. "And Sherlock Holmes?"

"He is coming," I say. "I assure you."

Henry Baskerville nods. "A dram, Dr. Mortimer? I know I've already had my morning dose, but—"

"I think a dram is most certainly in order," Dr. Mortimer says, taking the teacup from Sir Henry. "Return to your room, and I'll bring one forthwith. Perkins, see that no one disturbs the body. And Barrymore," he eyes the frightened servant who cowers by the leaded glass doors. "As I said, I would speak with you about why this unfortunate man is wearing your clothes. But first, you must go and fetch the constable."

Barrymore nods and flees into the shadows of the house.

Dr. Mortimer turns toward me. "It might be best if you write to Sherlock Holmes again, Dr. Watson. This affair seems to have taken quite a turn."

I hurry to my room and do as Dr. Mortimer requests, dashing off a letter to Holmes, mentioning only the second murder. Nothing of the occurrences in the cave. Nothing of the mannequin. Holmes, you really must come at once. I confess I no longer know how to proceed.

# 7

Making my way along the moorland road to the Grimpen post office, I pause beside the megalith to peer between its standing stones. Someone has placed flowers on the granite altar. Purple marsh orchid, yellow-rattle, and a most ethereal gathering of dog violet. I wonder about the meaning of the flowers as I draw the brown bottle of laudanum from my coat pocket and take a sip. I must calm myself. Order my thoughts.

*I'll speak with Barrymore upon my return to Baskerville Hall. (His cock in my mouth. I cannot stop thinking of it. The weight of the shaft. The taste of his hot ejaculate. It was all I'd wanted. And yet I was not like myself. I took no true pleasure in the act. Barrymore and I behaved more like the pale cave creatures than men, shifting about in the listless dark. And now what is to be done?)*

*I must also speak with Beryl Stapleton to discover what she knows of Hugo Baskerville's book. And more importantly, perhaps, I must attempt to discern why she does not trust my investigation.*

*Then there is still the matter of Lord V of Laughter Hall. He who keeps a telescope on the roof of his manor house may have seen either murder from that vantage point.*

*

I take a final look at the Neolithic altar where cut flowers (or are they offerings?) flutter in the breeze. Then I continue on my way.

In the grassy town square of Grimpen Village, a great bonfire is being laid for what I assume to be the harvest festival indicated to me by the postmaster. Plunged into the soil around the bonfire are what appears to be a series of ancient, possibly Roman, swords. They look like trophies of some kind. The swords are decorated with yellow rowan leaves and dark elderberries that glisten like blood in the light of the afternoon sun. A matronly woman sings an old song as she sprinkles the firewood with oil from a clay urn.

"Druids..." the postmaster says after I've handed him my message for Holmes and enquired about the bonfire and its attendant swords. "They were the ancient inhabitants of the moor. And many of us here in Grimpen are descended from those noble folk. We keep up the rituals now as a means of remembrance. But we are all good Christians here, I assure you. You really must come and see for yourself tomorrow, Doctor."

"Yes, I suppose I should." It occurs to me I might ask Barrymore if he would like to attend the festival with me. Perhaps, in that way, something could be mended between the two of us. If anything needs mending. All of it is so confusing. "Can you get this letter to London by this afternoon?"

The postmaster glances over the rim of his spectacles at the address. "Certainly. There's a train in half an hour. Every modern convenience, sir. Even here in the wilds of Dartmoor."

I consult a map in the post office and locate Merripit House, where Beryl Stapleton and her brother, the naturalist, are staying. It's not far off the moorland road, and I decide I'll speak with Miss Stapleton before returning to Baskerville Hall.

I make my way out of Grimpen Village and then onto a narrow road of silt and sand.

In the distance, clouds rise like the towers of some mysterious city. A flock of Grayface sheep grazes on the moor.

Merripit House sits on a low rise above the mire. It's a medieval peasant's cottage built of Dartmoor granite, rectangular in shape. My first thought when I catch sight of it is no one lives in this place... no one could live here. For the cottage is in shambles. Overgrown with dark ivy. Windowless. And, in places, the thatched roof has collapsed entirely.

The door of the house stands ajar, and I approach with care. "Miss Stapleton?" I say, tapping lightly on the weathered frame.

When there's no response, I push the door open and look inside.

The large main room is dim. And I believe it is made dimmer still because the walls have been painted black. Their surfaces appear to move subtly, shifting and fluttering, as if covered in some kind of tattered paper.

I step over the threshold, opening the door wide enough to let in the light.

It is then I realize the walls inside Merripit House are not papered. No. Every surface is, in fact, covered in wooly black butterflies. A hideous living tapestry. They shudder and shift, making an awful sound.

In the center of the broken hardwood floor is a long low mound the size of a human body, and it too crawls with black butterflies.

I steel my nerves and take a step toward the mound, intent on discovering what rests beneath the layer of insects.

My shoe must cause some board to shift, for suddenly, a small decayed hutch topples over, making a loud bang. And at that moment, every butterfly in the room takes flight, filling the air with black wings.

One of the creatures darts into my mouth, fluttering against my tonsils, causing me to gag. Another flies directly into my eye.

I spit and bat at the fluttering shapes in horror, spinning about, trying to find the door. When I finally do, I scurry from the house and run directly into Beryl Stapleton herself.

She doesn't falter. Nor does she even seem surprised by my presence. If anything, she grows more serene at the sight of me. She's no longer dressed in the robe covered in crescent moons. Now, she wears a simple black dress with pearl buttons at the sleeves and breast. Her dark hair is undone from its pins and falls gracefully down the length of her back.

"Dr. Watson," she says. "How good of you to visit." She reaches out and delicately plucks a black butterfly from my lapel. Then she holds the wriggling thing upside down as if to study it. "Clyclopides. My brother tells me they are rare in the South of England. But I'm afraid we've developed quite an infestation here at the house."

"Miss Stapleton, what is the meaning of this?"

"Meaning?"

"Yes," I reply, growing angry. "You are obscuring a great deal. Nothing is playing out as it should."

Beryl Stapleton releases the Clyclopides. It flutters up into the air. "Isn't it?" she says lightly.

"You must tell me exactly what's going on. Tell me this minute."

She smiles. "I can do better than that, Doctor. I'll show you."

With that, she lifts her hand and positions it in front of my face, pressing the tip of her middle finger to her thumb. Her plum-colored nails glisten in the afternoon light.

She snaps her fingers then. And the effect is immediate. The grassy landscape of the moor turns suddenly upside-down. Sky becomes earth. Earth becomes sky. And a terrible spinning ensues. End over end. Sky and earth. Earth and sky.

And suddenly, shockingly, I am no longer on the moor.

I'm standing in the large sitting room of 221B Baker Street, the apartment where Holmes and I have kept house for some twenty-odd years. The room, like the rural landscape, seems to spin. My knees weaken. I feel as though I might collapse. I cover my eyes and stifle a scream.

In an instant, then, all is calm. Baker Street is as it should be. As it has always been. And though I am frightened by the method of my arrival, part of me is terribly relieved to be home.

A warm fire crackles in the hearth. The air smells of sweet tobacco. All the old landmarks are in place. The chemical corner and the deal-topped table. The violin case. The pipe rack. Here is the jackknife stabbed through a pile of unanswered letters. And here, the closet filled with Holmes's disguises—the sailor, the aged book collector, the Italian priest.

I steady myself and look toward the two velvet armchairs facing the fire. One chair belongs to me, of course. And the other to Holmes. Together, we engaged in many a late night of stimulating conversation from these perches.

Memories creep back. Quiet interludes. Lovely things.

Holmes's chair appears to be occupied at the moment. I see the top of a man's head. Dark hair, well-groomed.

Without announcing myself, I step forward, hoping to surprise my old friend. Perhaps wishing all the trouble between us might miraculously dissipate.

It is then I hear a soft wet sound.

As I round the edge of the bearskin rug, I see Holmes seated himself on the velvet cushion. His dressing gown has fallen open, and he is naked beneath. Long pale torso. Every muscle etched. The widow's peak of his hairline seems all the more severe. Holmes's bare legs are spread. And kneeling between them is a man dressed in common work clothes. A chimney sweep, perhaps. Or someone who sells apples on the street corner.

The man is mustached. Jowled. Average looking in every way. And he is sucking vigorously at Holmes's swollen cock. He holds the detective's testicles in one hand, tugging at them gently as he slides the fingers of the other hand up and down Holmes's shaft.

I watch in horror as the workman moves his tongue around the head, greedily lapping at its pinkish flesh.

Holmes utters a soft, contented sigh. I know the sound well. For many years, I evoked such sighs from him. But in the months prior to my departure for Baskerville Hall, all of that—decades of companionship and adventure—fell to pieces. I cannot say there was a single cause. Instead, a string of silences and misunderstandings. Petty arguments. In the end, Holmes simply said he no longer cared for me in the way I cared for him.

You must have realized it, Watson. Even you could make such an obvious deduction, I should think.

I had wept. He had not. I pleaded with him to reconsider. But he would hear nothing of it.

The Adventure of Baskerville Hall was to be our final case together.

But who will write your stories? I asked.

Holmes had looked at me pityingly. How often must I tell you I don't like your stories, Watson. They are quite... unnecessary.

Here by the fire, the Great Detective opens his eyes, gray and drowsy beneath a heavy brow.

He places one hand upon the workman's head to still the man's bobbing and peers at me. "What are you doing here?" he says as if he's waking from a dream. "You're supposed to be in Dartmoor."

"Holmes—" I begin but do not know what to say. How to explain.

Then a voice in my ear. Beryl Stapleton. "Not this, Doctor. Never this again." And I hear the snap of her fingers once more.

The room spins even more vigorously this time, causing my gorge to rise.

And I am no longer before the hearth on Baker Street. Instead, I fall to my knees on a soft green island in the Grimpen Mire.

The bog is all around me. Furze and peat and bramble. There is no path here. I am stranded in the forbidden land where Hugo Baskerville saw the pony die. The bog is like quicksand in many places, Dr. Mortimer said. There are islands of firm ground, but all the rest is ready to devour an unexpecting traveler.

Rain falls, a cold October drizzle. White mist rises from the peat.

I find I cannot escape the image of Holmes and the workman. It's like a boot heel grinding away at my heart.

All my love has been dragged out of me. Strewn about like so much waste.

Twenty years of cozy gas light, Mrs. Hudson's dinners, and running about like boys in the fog. Twenty years of games afoot.

Now I am an old man. A foolish man.

How did Beryl Stapleton undo all logic in the briefest of moments with the snap of her painted fingers? As if to remind me nothing in my aging soul is real. Nothing has ever been real. Not space or time or love.

It's then I hear a sound from the bog. A long low cry. Mournful, it swells, rising finally to a howl. It is the same sound I heard last evening by the megalith. Only this time, it's much closer.

Something rustles the sedges before me, and I know I must flee. I must find my way to the road, to safety.

I spot a nearby island of firm ground and leap to it, avoiding the quicksand of the bog. I draw my pistol from my pocket.

The cry comes again. A keening.

I turn to look. And there in the mists, I see... how do I describe it?

It is not a dog.

No.

It is sometimes a dog. A large grayish hound with muscled flanks and a menacing jaw.

But it will not hold its shape. Soon it is like a man. Lean and strong with wiry hair. The man ambles on hands and feet, turning his head in the mist. Left and then right. Perhaps scenting the air. Searching for prey.

Now he has a doggish face. Long muzzle. Pointed ears.

And even as I watch, the figure folds and changes once again. Swelling and contracting like a lung. It is a rent in the air. A dark wound that opens and closes. I see a dog and a man inside the wound. I see two dogs. I see two men. They embrace. They are all tangled. They lift their heads and howl at the dead gray sky.

I raise my pistol, trembling.

The wound opens further, folding back its edges like lips. And the wound looks at me.

Hound of the Baskervilles.

Hound of us all.

Eyes like dark fissures. Holes that blot out the sky.

Then a ravening scream.

And it runs like a dog and a man and a wound.

Howling, mad.

I stumble backward, trying to flee. And suddenly, I am no longer on the island. I am neck-deep in the bog itself. I struggle, trying to find purchase in the peat. But the bog shifts, sucking at me. Drawing me down.

All firmness breaks away.

Fetid water flows into my mouth. My nose. I cough and spit. But there is still more water. Bitter taste.

And I feel the shadow over me.

God of Hell. Swelling and collapsing. Jaws shining. Eyes red.

It stares down at me.

Old man and dying man. All alone.

Water in my mouth. Water in my throat. I cry out, choking.

# 8

A gasp of breath, and the light leaks in.

A coughing fit forces dark water from my lungs. I am bog drenched, lying on my back. Shivering, cold.

But I am not dead.

I am not dead.

A face appears and hovers over mine, hazy in the light. I feel a rush of panic and want to scream. For it's an animal. The creature from the mire.

No.

It's a Grayface sheep, chewing a mouthful of fibrous cud. The sheep regards me with a placid expression, and I wince at the sour smell of its breath.

I am no longer trapped in the bog. This is the flat dim plain of the moor. Wind moves the tall grass. Dark clouds churn overhead. I have no idea how I arrived at this place. Perhaps Beryl Stapleton transported me once again. (Snap of her fingers. Flash of lightning.)

> *Where is the beast that pursued me? Dog that is not a dog. Man that is not a man.*

I reach for my pistol, but the weapon is no longer in my pocket. I curse, for I must have dropped it when I fell into the swamp.

I find the bottle of laudanum instead blessedly intact. And I press weakly at the cork until it falls away. I lift the bottle to my lips and take a sip. A single dose is not enough; I suckle sweet liquid, mouthful after mouthful, until the bottle yields no more. Only afterward, as I wipe at my lips, do I begin to understand how much opium I likely ingested.

*Thoughts are dragged back to the bog. The creature that swelled and contracted like a lung. Impossible thing. And what I saw in London too. The workman pleasuring Holmes. And worse than that—Holmes's face. The face I know so well. I saw the way he looked at me. As if I was a summer fly, snuck in through the window at Baker Street, needing to be swatted. And there was something else as well. Something I could not have guessed until I saw it in his drowsy gray eyes. Sherlock Holmes, the Great Detective, Savior in a Deerstalker Cap, had no intention of coming to Dartmoor. This final case was not a case at all. It was a ruse. A means of ridding himself of a most distasteful problem.*

*I should have realized something was amiss. Holmes only takes on cases that compel him. So very few, in fact. When a scenario actually engages his obsessive, analytical mind, he throws himself at it with the greatest ferocity. He's never sent me out alone before, for what would be the point? In his opinion, I'd miss all the facts. I'd botch the thing before we'd even begun.*

*The truth was I'd been sent to Dartmoor not to start an investigation, but so Holmes would no longer have to look at me.*

*When I finally return to London, he'll be in absence. Mrs. Hudson will explain in her kind, apologetic tone that the master has been called away for a month or two. And I will quietly pack my things (dog that I am) and move to some vacant room in Piccadilly.*

*No more begging. No more tiresome demonstrations of emotion. Holmes will finally be rid of me.*

*Yet what he does not realize, of course, is he has made a terrible mistake. Perhaps the worst of his career. For there is something profound here in Dartmoor. Something out there in the bog. This is not some simple case of secret love or stolen jewelry. This is a shining thing. Numinous. A beast in the darkness. Like those mysteries of the ancient past. Eleusis and Samothrace. Youths drawn down into caves. Holy monsters grinning in the torchlight. I believe whatever pattern is emerging here might finally be a match for the sacred dimensions of Holmes's intellect.*

*Mysterium Tremendum. Mystery as Revelation.*

*And yet he does not see. He will not see because he is so lost in his intentions.*

As I consider all of this, the laudanum begins to take hold. Thoughts slide one into the next. My limbs grow heavy.

I attempt to roll over onto my stomach, but my body is slow to respond. Too much opium in the blood. And the shock of nearly drowning.

I rock back and forth. Finally, half turning, I try to stand but find I cannot. So instead, I crawl, moving on hands and knees. Dripping dark water onto stalks of purple heather.

*Everyone at Baskerville Hall expects the arrival of Sherlock Holmes. Great sense-maker. Architect in the ruins. And yet I understand now they will never have Holmes. Instead, they have Dr. Watson. But the question arises: Do they even have Dr. Watson? Or were they sent some drug-addled clown? Broken-hearted thing. Old man and dying man. No match for this reckoning upon the moor.*

I continue to crawl, placing one hand in front of the other. Just as I crawled through the deserts of Maiwand, some fifty miles west of Candahar, surrounded by the men of my brigade. I kept my head down, yet I was struck in the shoulder by a bullet from an Afghan jezail. A wound opened. Bleeding. Ragged. Did it ever really close?

*Barrymore (beautiful boy) was wrong when he said there are no clues in this place. For nearly everything begins to seem like a clue, green and phosphorescent in the hazy light.*

*This rock, for instance. A piece of granite. It reminds me of my boyhood in Edinburg. Skipping stones on the lake with my old friend (what was his name... why can't I remember?) He was taller than me. Fine long limbs. A superior face. His father worked as a draftsman. We laughed together. Talked for many hours.*

*And this grass. Like my mother's skirts. Swaying as she crosses the parlor floor. She strokes my hair. Tells me I am good. How long has it been since someone told me such a thing?*

*Here is a piece of wood. The old structures. Buildings not yet fallen.*

*And here, a patch of yellow gorse. Every flower is like a mouth. An open jaw.*

I look over my shoulder to make sure nothing follows me. Dog that is not a dog. Man that is not a man. But the moor is empty as far as the eye can see.

I continue to crawl, hand-over-hand, now thinking of this case that is not a case.

There is a Hound, yes. Or something like a Hound. A figure that stalks and cries and changes its shape every moment of its infernal life. But how can I even begin to explain to anyone what I saw?

*A realization: I must find a way to answer my own questions if I am to be here all alone—if I am to always be alone. Yet the more I think about this mystery, the more it seems itself like a mire.*

*So soft in places. Ready to swallow a man.*

*The yellowed book (Sir Hugo's devil book). Dr. Mortimer and his mannequin. Henry Baskerville and poor beautiful Barrymore. There must be some line of inquiry. Some way to set us all free.*

I try to imagine how Holmes would proceed. But I do not know how he proceeds. No matter how many times I've watched the conjuring trick of his deductions, the illusion remains obscure.

*Slashes across the face of the moon. The engraving on the phallus of the mannequin (satyrs dancing about a fire). The painting of the hunched creature in the natatorium. Ruined city of a ruined Hell.*

*Certainly, all of it must mean something. And yet it seems now like so much nonsense.*

*I hear Beryl Stapleton's laughter. The sound is only in my mind, but its effect is no less painful.*

*For what can I do to protect anyone? They are all innocents, are they not? I must resume my search with vigor. Assemble the facts. But what if there are only monstrosities here? Occulted things. Forever hidden.*

*Baskerville Hall rises in the distance. Black ship upon a blacker sea. And am I not adrift as well? No. I cannot be adrift. For if there is to be no Sherlock Holmes, it's left for me to steer this ship.*

*Yet I am not a detective. No part of me is a detective.*

*(For what is a detective but a boy's invention? An adventurer's game. And I am through with games. Finished with pretending to be what I am not and living as I should not.)*

I gaze up at the great dark house, the high stony walls and the black towers pressing at the sky. And it is then I am stopped, as if by some powerful yet invisible hand.

At first, I do not understand what has compelled me to pause. Then I see a figure standing at the mullioned window of the house's southern tower. A large man. Grave and still. He watches my slow progress across the moor with bleak interest.

I crawl closer, trying to get a better look. Bog water drips from my brow, momentarily blurring my vision. I wipe at it, desperate to see.

The man's face hovers there in the darkness of the window, flesh swollen, nearly putrescent as if some gross malignancy lurks beneath his skin. His hair is long, hideously tangled. Even in the light of the sun, it is dim. And there is something wrong with his eyes as well. Something I cannot quite understand. They look too full somehow. Ready to burst. Like spider's eggs.

The man leans forward, placing one large hand on the windowsill. He's studying me, this behemoth, this stranger. Yes, a stranger. For he is certainly no one I have encountered before.

Meaning there is someone else in the house, Watson. Holmes's voice says inside my head. Someone you have yet to discover. Pay attention now. This man presents an answer of sorts. Or at least a probable question.

As I watch, the large man opens his mouth as if to show the shape of his lower teeth. Then he lets his tongue loll out. A fat dark tongue.

I think at first the stranger might mean to call out. But he makes no sound. He just stands there with his mouth open, tongue hanging obscenely. He leers at me with his bulging eyes.

He sees me.

The game, as Holmes would say, is afoot. But this does not feel like a game. This feels like something wretched and cold. Like something crawling out here on the moor. Shivering. Waiting to die.

I watch the man. The stranger. His eyes swollen. Tongue hanging. And I know he intends something terrible.

I crawl faster. And faster still.

# 9

I use the granite column on the portico of Baskerville Hall to pull myself into a standing position. Then, stumbling forward, I throw open the oaken door and stagger into the empty foyer over the threshold. My suit is dripping wet. Shoes full of bog water and pockets lined with mud. I lean against the wainscot, attempting to steady myself.

I know my purpose. I must find the stranger in the tower. Stop him from committing whatever horror he intends.

I take a breath and reach for my pistol. But of course, there is no pistol to be found. I must search for a weapon. I dare not confront the giant without some means of defense.

I enter the parlor where I had my first interview with Dr. Mortimer. After tripping over a low table and knocking it on its side, I discover a veritable medieval armory hanging on the far wall. Barbs and spears and long-handled swords, all protruding like rays of the sun from the Baskerville coat of arms.

I attempt to pry a ceremonial broadsword from its fastenings, but having no luck with that, I select a primitive sort of mace—two smooth stones tethered to a wooden shaft. Hefting the thing, I momentarily imagine as if I've been transformed into some Neolithic barbarian. But when I catch a glimpse of myself in a gilded wall mirror, the illusion is shattered, for I look like nothing more than an overfed Londoner wielding an old stick.

Undeterred, I turn from the mirror and call out for Dr. Mortimer. Even in my stupor, I understand finding the southern tower in this infernal labyrinth will be much easier with him at my side.

When there's no response in the lower halls, I ascend the darkened stair and call out once more.

The door of Henry Baskerville's room opens a crack, and the baronet, eyelids heavy with sleep, peers out. "My God," he says, surveying my ruined clothes. "What's happened?"

"Please stay in your room, Sir Henry," I say. "I believe there's an intruder in the house."

"The witch again?"

"No. A man in the southern tower."

Sir Henry opens the door wider. He's barefoot, still in his nightshirt. Behind him, the priapic mannequin rests placidly in its chair.

"Do you know where I might find Dr. Mortimer?" I ask.

"He's gone off to Grimpen Village with the constable. They've taken the body. I can show you the way to the tower, though."

"I don't want to put you in any danger."

Sir Henry rubs his eyes and straightens his back. "Cousin Charles would have wanted me to be strong. And the fact of the matter is I'm tired of remaining in my room, Dr. Watson. We Baskervilles have been defending this land since before the writing of the Domesday Book." He glances at my mace. "At any rate, it looks like I'll be well protected."

"All right," I say. "Take me to the tower. But we must proceed with caution."

The baronet nods. "Just let me find my slippers first."

Sir Henry guides me down a series of long dark corridors to a staircase that opens onto a square balustraded gallery. The stonework here is exposed and of a cruder nature than the rest of the house. There's a smell of must and decay. "Stuffy old place, isn't it?" Sir Henry says. "This is the original section of Baskerville Hall. Built during the reign of Elizabeth and sealed off by my Uncle Rodger. Charles told me there's quite a large family of long-eared bats living in the rafters."

I duck my head and follow the baronet over piles of crumbling masonry, moving past a series of disused rooms filled with cobwebs and dust. Thankfully no winged vermin makes an appearance. There are, however, quite a few scuttling fleshy-tailed rats as well as a frightened moorland stoat who seems to have lost his way in these dark passages.

At the end of a dim hall, we come to a clock in a long case. Instead of numbers, the moon's phases are inscribed upon its silvery face. "It's good you asked me about the tower, actually," Sir Henry says. "The entrance is well concealed. I'm not sure even Dr. Mortimer knows where to find it." He reaches up and moves the single iron hand of the clock to point at the full moon. (The many-eyed moon). Some hidden latch releases, causing a portion of the wall to swing open like a door.

"Hugo Baskerville is said to have used the tower as his

private sanctuary," Sir Henry says. "It's where he conducted his... I suppose you might call them his rituals. It's been abandoned since that time. Charles always said old Hugo left an evil residue."

"Evil indeed," I say, gazing up into the shadows of the stair and hefting my mace.

Sir Henry moves to step into the alcove, and I reach out and touch his arm. "It's not safe."

He looks suddenly willful. "If someone is intruding in my home, Dr. Watson, I want to see his face."

I realize I cannot prevent the baronet from moving about in his own house. And at any rate, I'm feeling steadier on my feet. I'll be capable of providing the necessary protection. Or that is what I tell myself, at least.

I lead, and Sir Henry follows, ascending the winding tower stair. A clattering sound issues from somewhere above, and I pause to listen.

"What did he look like, the man you saw?" Sir Henry whispers.

I picture the vast figure hovering in the gloom of the tower window. "A tangle of long black hair," I say. "And very large in his stature. Nearly a giant."

"I don't know anyone of that description."

"No. He was quite unusual."

At the top of the stairs, we find a stone room in utter disarray—vellum pages torn from antique volumes, a threadbare settee upended, and iron boxes broken of their locks.

"It looks as though someone was searching for something," Sir Henry says, moving papers with his slippered foot. "These are peerage charts. Lists of cousins and half-cousins and all the rest. I knew they were stored somewhere in the house."

The clattering sound issues again from a second room leading off from the first.

I motion for Sir Henry to get behind me as I grip the handle of my mace and approach the door.

Inside, we encounter a scene that belongs in one of Dante's levels of Hell. This room has been ransacked—but worse than that, the bodies of some ten or fifteen mangled carrion crows are strewn about. Their wings are broken. Pinions torn. Blood is spread across the flagstones in great wheeling arcs. Some of the birds have been dismembered entirely. A head here. A curled talon there.

The sole avian survivor stands on an ornately carved table, sorting through detritus with his woody, black beak. He was the apparent cause of the clattering sound, and he seems oblivious to the state of his mangled brethren.

As I step toward the crow, he cries out and takes flight, exiting through the open tower window into the rain. It is the very window from which the stranger watched me crawl across the moor. But there is no sign of him now. The tower room is empty.

I wonder, Watson, Holmes's voice speaks up inside my head. Is it possible you hallucinated that man? You wanted a solution so badly that you invented one.

But I refuse to doubt my senses.

More than that, I refuse to listen to Sherlock Holmes any longer. Even an imagined version of him.

"Poor birds," Sir Henry says, looking down at the body

of a crow that seems to have been turned inside out. "Who would do such a thing?"

"I'm sure I don't know." I peer into the flat black eye of another dead crow.

The room itself is circular in shape and at its center is a kind of raised wooden platform supporting a rotted, straw-stuffed bed.

"This was where Hugo Baskerville slept?"

"Not slept," Sir Henry replies. "He brought his conquests into this room. The youths of Grimpen village and... other things if the legend is to be believed."

"The Hound." I think of the creature in the bog and wonder if I should attempt to describe what I saw to Sir Henry. I decide against it. Such a revelation would only serve to further inflame his condition. Instead, I glance out the tower window. The stones of the Neolithic henge stand darkly in the rain. I can just make out the granite altar from this distance. "Whoever was up here can't have gotten far," I say. "We must search the house."

Sir Henry looks vaguely surprised by this suggestion. "The whole house?"

"Yes."

"Well, I don't think I've ever even seen the whole house."

"What do you mean?"

"When we were boys, Charlie and I spent an entire summer trying to draw a map of the place. But no matter how many drafts we made, the map never came out right. We always found something new. Hidden passages. Chambers built on top of chambers. There's an alley for tenpin, a garden with no doors, and a room with a floor covered in African sand. I haven't been able to locate any of that again. Not since I was very young." Sir Henry pauses, growing thoughtful. "Once, when we were eleven or twelve, Charlie told me he'd started to believe every room in the house was repeated at least once. He said he'd seen two parlors and two dining rooms. That's why it couldn't be mapped. A ridiculous idea, of course. But if this man of yours has escaped the tower, I don't think we'll find him easily."

I nod, wondering how much more misaligned with reality this could become. Speaking with Sir Henry was like taking part in some controlled hallucination. "We must post a lookout," I say firmly. "Remain vigilant."

The baronet has begun to seem feeble and sunken once more. The dream of adventure has ended. He is no longer the Celtic warrior set on defending his land. "Perhaps you merely saw one of the stablemen Perkins employs," he says. "They sometimes roam about for various reasons."

"Perhaps," I say, though I do not believe the figure I saw was a stableman for a moment. "I'll check the rooms in the old wing at least. It might be best if you return to your quarters now."

Sir Henry nods, looking as if he needs another dram. Thankfully, he doesn't ask about Holmes's arrival.

I do not want to lie to the poor man.

# 10

*Here I shall pause this record, my semblance of a narrative, to put thoughts in better order. Perhaps it's because the opium is finally leaving my blood that I can see with greater clarity.*

*Old structures (for better or worse) rise again.*

*First, I should say this set of notes now belongs entirely to me. I'll no longer gather a daily report for Sherlock Holmes. After the look I saw on his face in London, I realize he's likely been tossing my unopened correspondences into a cheerfully crackling fire.*

*Still, this log must be maintained to organize the case's facts. For even in a sobered state, my mind does not serve as such a ready catalog as that of the Great Detective. I cannot recall the required array of facts at will. So this gathering of pages will henceforth act as a kind of memory. And if I am successful in finding a solution, I may extract a "Dr. Watson Mystery" from it. The first of its kind. I'll submit my story humbly to The Strand. Who knows if they would publish such a thing, but I owe it to myself to try.*

*And I must admit the idea of Holmes coming across it at the newsstand gives me the greatest of pleasures.*

*But first, toward a solution...*

*As Sir Henry predicted, all the dim and dusty rooms of the old wing were empty. There was no stranger to be found, no mad giant lurking in the shadows. Where he has gone, I cannot begin to imagine. So now I am left to plot my next move on this most disordered chessboard.*

*I shall call upon Lord V of Laughter Hall before the day is through. It's high time I spoke to the reclusive inventor about what he might have seen through his telescope.*

*Before that, I must speak with Barrymore. His reaction to the body in the Yew Alley was of interest, and of course, the corpse appeared to be wearing his clothes. There are other subjects to discuss with him as well. Much more difficult in nature.*

After a wash and a change of clothes, I find the young servant seated alone in the formal dining room at the long ebony table. He's lit a single taper in a brass candelabra and stares fixedly at its flame. His eyes are coal-colored. Skin pale. His workman's hands, too large for his frame, rest before him on the lacquered surface. I think of how those hands caressed me in the shadows of the cave, rough and calloused against my soft flesh. The taste of him, like the moor itself. Wind and heather. The darkness of the sky. "Barrymore?" I say.

He glances at me, no longer appearing afraid exactly but rather weary.

"Are you all right?"

He returns his gaze to the candle. "No, sir. I am not."

"You needn't call me 'sir,' you know," I say, approaching the table. "Not after all this."

"I must, I fear. It's in my nature."

"Very well. Call me whatever you like. Can I sit with you?" He nods, and I take a seat in the tall black chair to his left. "Why are you looking at the candle?"

"My mother told me if I ever find myself distressed and I do not know how to proceed, I should stare at the tip of a flame for an hour," Barrymore says. "It's meant to calm the mind."

"Is it working?"

"Not in this case."

I look at the tip of the candle flame myself, the way it dances. It reminds me of the weird, bright eyes of the creature in the bog, and I find I must look away.

"Barrymore, I want to talk to you about the man who—"

"You needn't prompt me with your questions, sir. I'll tell you plainly."

"All right."

"The man killed in the Yew Alley was called Seldon."

I recognize the name. Dr. Mortimer mentioned it to me in our first interview. Seldon was the escaped convict from Princetown prison who was thought to be hiding somewhere on the moor. I presented him as a possible suspect to Holmes in my initial letter. "The Notting Hill Murderer?" I say.

"I am not sure if he was a murderer, sir."

"What do you mean?"

"I didn't know him long. A month and a few days. I met him on the moor one morning. He was hungry and cold. He had only his prisoner's rags for clothes."

"So you gave him some of your clothing."

Barrymore nods. "And food from the house. Kindling for a fire. I knew it wasn't right. But so many things are not right here."

"Why would you have treated this man with such kindness when you understood the reprehensible crimes he'd been convicted of?"

Barrymore looks at me again, and I do not need to hear a response to understand. It's there in his depthless eyes. "I don't have friends in this house, sir," he says. "Not even Perkins talks to me. He keeps to himself and his drink. And because I serve the Baskervilles, the people of Grimpen avoid me as though I am diseased."

"They remember the history of Sir Hugo, do they?"

"As if it happened yesterday," Barrymore says. "So I do my chores. And when I am not doing my chores, I sit alone in my room."

"But you must have family."

"My father is dead. My mother, gone away."

I pause. "This Seldon, the convict, he provided—"

"Kindnesses," Barrymore says. "I liked his stories. He was a sailor in his youth. He once saw mermaids swimming just off his cargo ship's starboard side. He said they had the gray skin of porpoises, but their skin was decked in rubies and emeralds. All shining in the sun. Can you imagine that, sir?"

"I cannot."

Barrymore squints at the flame. "Seldon was a lonely man as well."

I want to ask what kindnesses beyond stories of mermaids the convict provided. I suppose I'd wanted to believe that what happened between the two of us in the cave was unique. An awakening for Barrymore, despite our altered states. But why should it be? It certainly wasn't new to me.

"Do you know who murdered this man," I say, "this Seldon?"

"I didn't even know he would be coming to the house

last night," Barrymore replies. "He only did such a thing a few times before. He'd tap on the glass doors that lead onto the Yew Alley when hungry. I would go to him and—" He breaks off.

"I'm sorry."

He presses one hand to his face.

"And I'm sorry for what happened in the cave," I say. "It was so... sudden. We didn't have the chance to speak."

"Why would you be sorry?"

"Because, well, as you said, the fissure made you feel odd. It made me feel odd as well. And I wasn't sure if—"

"It didn't make me feel that odd."

"And the thing that happened between us?"

"As I said, sir, I am lonely."

I reach across the table toward his hand but do not take it. "I'm lonely too."

"You're from London, though."

"A man can be lonely anywhere."

"Well, I don't want to live like this anymore."

"No. I don't want that for you either, Barrymore. I want you safe. When I saw the body in the Yew Alley, I believed it was you. I thought I'd failed to protect you."

"You're a kind man."

"I am a confused man. And a foolish man most of the time. But I am not going to be foolish in this case. There's a festival in Grimpen Village tomorrow."

"The Harvest Fair," Barrymore says.

"That's right. Here's what I propose. You're going to accompany me to the Harvest Fair. We'll say I need your assistance in some matter. But when we arrive in Grimpen Village, we will not attend the festival. Instead, I'll put you on a train to London."

Barrymore's eyes widen.

"The only way to truly protect you is to remove you from this dreadful situation entirely."

"But where will I go in London? I have never been to that place."

I think of the picture book I saw in his room, London for a Day: Scenes of the City. "I'll give you an address, that of the Diogenes Club. It was founded by an acquaintance of mine, Mycroft Holmes. I cannot call him a friend, but I know him well enough, and he wields great power. You'll say my name to the doorman at the club. Tell him you're to be given rooms. And the doorman will comply. Mycroft Holmes owes me certain favors."

"You would use one of your favors for me?"

"I would do more than that. But I'm afraid I must also ask for something in return."

"What is it?"

"We are going to make sure no one else is harmed this evening. I have reason to believe there's a man in the house. An intruder."

"The man with the dragging step?" Barrymore says.

"I don't know exactly. But I think it will be best if we stand guard tonight. You won't be in any danger. I'll be with you. I have some experience with such posts because of my time in Candahar."

"Yes, sir. I'll be glad to stand with you."

"We'll both need weapons."

"There are hunting rifles in the stables. Perkins keeps them in working condition."

"Very good. Collect the rifles and meet me in the parlor after the sun goes down." I rise to leave.

"Thank you... Dr. Watson."

"You're quite welcome, Barrymore."

# 11

Laughter Hall lies some four miles to the north on a high and stony ridge. Perkins the groom, red-faced from gin, drives me in the wagonette along a rutted, winding road. He's wrapped in his cowled gray shawl, boney hands trembling from the cold.

I must yell to be heard over the strong wind blowing down from the highlands. "Did you notice anything out of the ordinary last evening?" I say, hoping Perkins could provide further insight about the identity of the stranger in the tower.

He whips feebly at the gray mare. "Orderly, sir? Everything is in order, yes."

"Out of the ordinary," I shout. "Odd noises? Anyone lurking in the shadows?"

"I don't see so well in the dark, sir."

"Did you hear anything?"

He shakes his head. "I don't hear so well, either. I go to bed early most evenings and sleep like the dead."

"You mentioned your wife yesterday," I say, searching for a more useful line of questioning.

"God rest her. It's been many years now."

"You told me she once found Hugo Baskerville's book in the house and nearly fainted because of it."

Perkins glances at me with bloodshot eyes. “His devil book.”

“Yes, his devil book. What exactly did your wife say she read in it?”

“Oh, she did not tell me. She said what was writ there was far too terrible to speak aloud.”

“And you have no idea what happened to the book after that?”

“My wife, she hid it away, sir. She said no one should read such things as she had read. And don’t ask me where she hid it. She kept very few secrets. But the location of Sir Hugo’s evil book was one of them.”

“Perhaps she confided in someone else?”

Perkins pulls at the reins to slow the horse as we approach a bend in the high road. “There were more people in the house then. His lordship, Sir Rodger, had a pretty wife, the Lady Arabella. And there was his mother, Old Madam, who walked with a silver-headed cane and put on such airs. Those women required a great many servants. Also, there was more money in those days due to Sir Rodger’s exploits in Africa.”

“How did Rodger Baskerville make his money in Africa?”

“I cannot say, sir. But there’s little doubt it was by some nefarious means.”

“Why nefarious?”

Perkins whips the horse more vigorously this time. “Because he was a Baskerville.”

“And you have no idea who might currently know the whereabouts of Sir Hugo’s book?”

"It has always struck me the Baskervilles know things beyond what they have been told."

I think back to Dr. Mortimer saying the Baskervilles possess certain "arcane knowledge."

"You believe Sir Henry knows where the book is?"

"It is his family's possession."

"And what of Beryl Stapleton?"

"The witch?"

"Is it possible she's found the book?"

"Anything is possible with that one," Perkins says. "Countrymen have seen her in the old henge. She keeps an odd company, sir."

"The young women with bog flowers in their hair and the men in leathers?"

Perkins nods. "They do not know their Bible. They abide by the old ways."

"Is it some kind of Druidic sect that gathers in the megalith?"

"I do not know what you might call such people as them."

"Well, is there anything else you can tell me, Perkins? Anything at all that might help me with this case?"

"I thought you were awaiting Mr. Holmes, sir."

I feel more than a little irritated by his comment. Even the old groom believes me to be incompetent. "I've decided I might as well try to work things out while I wait."

"According to your stories, Mr. Holmes wouldn't like that very much."

"You've read the stories in The Strand?" I'm startled Perkins is literate.

"Two or three, sir. Nearly everyone has read two or three."

"I suppose so..."

He's quiet for a time, then says: "There is one more thing, but please do not say I told it."

"Of course, I won't."

"I do not believe Dr. Mortimer is who he claims to be."

"He's the county physician. That's a verifiable fact."

"I think he is something else as well. He has interests in the house."

"Baskerville Hall?

Perkins nods. "He has designs upon it."

"What makes you believe such a thing?"

"I have seen him examining all manner of official papers since the death of Sir Charles. And twice he has spoken with a barrister."

"Dr. Mortimer would not be in line to inherit Baskerville Hall."

"He was very close with Sir Charles, sir. Very close indeed. And he is a clever man."

I am confused by the idea that Dr. Mortimer might have anything to do with the case, for it was he who called Holmes and me to Dartmoor. Why should he solicit an investigation if he was the one committing a crime?

Perkins raises his whip and points. "There it stands. Laughter Hall."

I gaze into the distance, expecting another brooding country manor of the same ilk as Baskerville Hall. But instead, I am greeted by what looks to be a replica of a medieval castle, complete with crenelated towers, a footbridge, and even a narrow water-filled moat.

I say replica here because Laughter Hall gives no real sense of age, nor does it even attempt authenticity.

It's not Gothic revival exactly, but almost some kind of Gothic parody with its exaggerated stonework and crossed swords hanging from the battlements.

It puts me in the mind of Horace Walpole's extravagant and rather queer paper mâché castle, Strawberry Hill. Walpole himself once said of the house that it was all "pretend observance and costumery." And that is exactly the impression evoked by Laughter Hall. It's as if I'm looking at a theater's false fronts and painted scenery, all constructed there upon the stony ridge. And I wonder why anyone would go to the trouble of creating such a frivolous eyesore in the middle of nowhere.

The wheels of the wagonette crunch along the house's drive, and we creak to a halt before the footbridge. "Thank you, Perkins," I say.

"Shall I wait for you, sir?"

"No. I'll find my own way back."

I cross the bridge as Perkins's cart clatters away, and I discover the wooden door of Laughter Hall bears an odd message rendered in gold paint: "WELCOME TRAVELER!" Certainly, a curious inscription for the home of a recluse.

Upon further examination, I realize there is no knocker on the door or even a handle of any kind.

I rap several times to no avail. Pressing my ear to the oak, I hear faint music. A tune I almost recognize. I inspect the permitter of the door frame, searching for a bell rope or some other device. But still, there's nothing. Frustrated, I gaze out over the greenish-gray expanse of the moor.

Beryl Stapleton was correct when she told me Lord V might have witnessed the murder of Sir Charles, for the high ridge provides an excellent vantage point. Baskerville Hall's Yew Alley is clearly visible. With the aid of a telescope, one could likely see every detail.

Speaking with Lord V seems all the more pressing now. But because he likely doesn't favor visitors merely dropping by, I realize I may have overestimated my chances for an audience.

As I consider searching for some kind of servant's entrance, a latch clicks behind me. I turn to see the painted door slowly open. Flickering light issues from within. The music is louder now. Low brass and a nervous skittering of violins. I recognize the melody. "Dream of a Witch's Sabbath" from Symphonie Fantastique. Holmes and I heard the piece performed several years ago from our box at the Royal Albert.

I step inside the foyer. The odd flickering light issues from some kind of magic lantern machine. An illuminated cylinder turns on a low table at the center of the room, projecting bright spirits and horned devils on the walls. They chase each other in a perpetual loop, loping fiendishly along.

Lord V is said to be some manner of an inventor, and this extravagant display in his foyer certainly fits the bill.

"Hello?" I call. "Is there anyone here?"

As if in response, another door opens in the wall just ahead.

"I am Dr. John Watson. I've come to ask you a few questions."

Spirits curl as the music swells.

Holmes once told me he believes people who live too long in the country become increasingly eccentric, eventually going half-mad. "They lose their capacity for rational thought, Watson. In the end, their gated houses and ivied walls are little more than prettily decorated mental wards."

As I pass through the second door, I find I must agree. For the inner chamber has a curiously mechanical aspect. There's some kind of track embedded in the floor, and sitting in the track is a small automated cart of the sort one might have found in the Pleasure Gardens at Vauxhall. I went there once with my mother when I was very young. We rode a little train through a Gypsum plaster tunnel decked in shimmering diamonds and sapphires made of sugar glass. In a whispered voice, my mother leaned down and said, "Look for the elves, John. They're surely hiding in these shadows." I looked but did not see. And I feel the same confusion here in Laughter Hall. For why would any man construct such a conveyance as this inside his house? I remember Beryl Stapleton saying she and her brother attended a rather theatrical dinner party at Laughter Hall. "All smoke and mirrors." Perhaps this is Lord V's rather unnatural method of entertaining his guests?

The door of the cart stands open and seeing no other recourse, I take a seat on the bench inside. I suppose if one wishes to talk with a profound eccentric, one must obey his whims.

As soon as I'm seated, the cart comes to life, lurching forward on its track, and a door in the far wall swings open. Somewhere, another phonograph begins to play. Not music now, but a man's voice. Crackling. Dramatic. "Down through the ages of time," the voice says. "Dartmoor has stood, a land of great mystery." The cart trundles into a room full of manmade fog. I take a handkerchief from my pocket and press it over my mouth and nose so as not to inhale too much of the stuff. In the distance then, the trumpeting call of some animal. A towering, long-necked shadow moves through the fog. And though I'm startled at first, I quickly realize at what I'm looking. I've seen bones in the Geological Wing of the Museum of Natural History: Iguanodon and Megalosaurus. And I understand something like a thunder lizard is being represented here. I'm inside some kind of large-scale mechanical diorama. Feathered palms emerge from layers of fog. There's a sound of running water, perhaps meant to approximate a prehistoric river.

As I observe the shadow of the great lumbering lizard, a leathery winged creature flies out of the fog toward the cart. Fearing an attack, I cry out and duck my head until I realize the beast is nothing more than an ingenious model attached to the ceiling by wires. The invention pulls away just as quickly as it came.

The cart continues through the primordial landscape, passing something that looks a great deal like the fissure I encountered in the cave beneath Baskerville Hall—a long narrow crack in the earth, glowing with an unnatural rose-colored light. "Great power has always resided here in Dartmoor," the voice on the phonograph continues.

Another door swings open, and the cart trundles into a large-scale replica of the moor itself, complete with yellow furze made of tatted wool and a painted gray sky. On a low hill, mechanical figures in hooded robes use a primitive system of pulleys to erect what I recognize as the standing stones of the megalith. The hood of one of the figures has fallen away, revealing the same blank wooden face as that of the priapic mannequin in Sir Henry's bedchamber. I wonder if Lord V helped construct the odd device for Dr. Mortimer's experiments.

The voice on the phonograph crackles to life again. "Ancient men understood the power of this land. Their magicians, known as Druids, came here to... came here to... came here to..." The voice suddenly cuts off. Lights dim and go out. I am left in darkness.

Somewhere above, a man screams.

"Hello? Are you all right?" I say. When there's no response, I exit the car, stumbling through the dark, hoping not to impale myself on some part of the diorama.

I pass through a tunnel into a half-lit room where a large model appears to depict the future of Dartmoor—an elaborate, sprawling cityscape with towers and crystalline pyramids. At the center stands a newly-fashioned megalith made of steel.

I hurry forward into a gallery of moorland artifacts: ancient weapons, geological formations, and the ivory skull of a prehistoric beast.

There's a door leading to a staircase. I ascend, and at the top of the stairs, a hatch opens onto the roof of the house. I step out into the blustery cold. The actual darkening moor sprawls all around. A figure stands at the crenelated roof's edge, looking out over the landscape. He wears some sort of dramatic costume, purple robes, and a red sash, like an emperor from some foreign land. He's balding. Only a gray fringe of longish hair remains.

"Your Lordship? I am Dr. John Watson. I work with Sherlock Holmes, and I'm wondering if I might ask you some questions."

He ignores me, gazing out at Baskerville Hall and the ring of standing stones beyond.

"Lord V, are you well? I heard someone cry out." I step forward and touch the man's shoulder. His body is oddly stiff, unmoving. I grip his arm and turn him toward me.

His brown eyes stare in horror. His jaw has been forced wide. Bloodied lips are drawn back, revealing broken teeth that scrape the sides of a brass telescope that's been thrust down his throat.

"Dear God, man! Can you breathe? Let me help you." I attempt to lower him to the ground, but his knees will not bend.

He stares at me a moment longer and then tries to speak. But rather than words issuing forth, blood bubbles up around the edges of the telescope, covering its lens and drooling down his chin.

"Hello?" I yell toward the open hatch. "Is there someone who can help us?"

But there is no response. The house is empty.

Finally, Lord V topples forward, dead in my arms.

## 12

In my twenty years of working with Sherlock Holmes, I've encountered a startling number of corpses. Parlor room poisonings. Drownings in the Thames. Brutal assaults in every district from Mayfair to Whitechapel. Once, man in Forest Row was pinned to a wall with a whaling harpoon. But the vicious and bizarre murder of Lord V of Laughter Hall weighs far more heavily than most. For it demonstrates a failure, undeniable. My dubious abilities in detection have cost yet another man his life.

Upon leaving Laughter Hall, I consider going directly to the constable in Grimpen Village. But the sun is setting, and I do not want to abandon Barrymore or Henry Baskerville. The moor and its environs grow increasingly dangerous by the hour. And I know I must maintain my post with the leering stranger from the southern tower likely roaming about in the shadows.

After a long walk back down the windswept highland road, I find Barrymore seated in the gaslit parlor of Baskerville Hall. He's dressed, not in his usual servant's uniform, but in a pair of rugged huntsman's trousers and a smart tweed vest. He looks, for all the world, like a young man on the cover of an adventure magazine. Crisp shirt sleeves rolled to reveal sinewed forearms. Black hair freshly oiled and slicked back from his high pale brow. Two long-barreled hunting rifles rest against the hearth, both within his capable reach.

"Sir," Barrymore says, rising from his seat. "What happened? Are you hurt?"

I shake my head, glancing down at my blood-streaked woolen suit. "Lord V of Laughter Hall. I found him on the roof of his house. He's been murdered."

"Lord V? But why?"

"I should confer with Dr. Mortimer."

"He hasn't returned from Grimpen Village. You look—you do not look well."

"I'll be fine, Barrymore."

"Let me help you, please." He steps forward, moving to take my coat. And perhaps it is due to my exhaustion or my heightened state of anxiety, but I find I can no longer contain my energies. Barrymore's strong narrow frame. His thoughtful eyes. The smell of hair tonic and lemon soap. Suddenly and with barely a conscious thought, I pull him close, putting my mouth to his.

Did we kiss in the cave beside the black fissure?

So much of that night is still lost to me.

But kissing him now feels wonderfully clean, as if I am drinking water from a secret moonlit spring. His lips are so full. Like memories. Days before the war. Before anything truly terrible ever happened. And to my surprise, Barrymore kisses me in return. His tongue in my mouth. His strong arms around my neck.

He pauses long enough to open his shirt, exposing a lean, hard chest. And I am pressing my lips to his taught skin as I attempt to shed my bloodstained garments.

He moves to unfasten my trousers, and though I desperately want to be naked with him, I still his hand and look toward the empty foyer, understanding Dr. Mortimer might walk through the door at any moment. "We shouldn't stay here," I whisper.

He holds my hand against his chest. I feel the quick patter of his heart. "I know a place we can go," he says, leading me into the foyer. We do not move toward his humble quarters at the back of the house nor ascend the stair to my room (which is certainly too close to Sir Henry's own). Instead, we hurry ever deeper, passing through the formal dining room where the long black table sits empty and then through the darkened portrait gallery where the painting of Hugo Baskerville glowers down at us.

We move through halls I have not yet seen, pausing shirtless in a dim corridor to press our bodies against one another. I kiss Barrymore's neck. He sighs into my ear. When we finally separate, I catch a glimpse of my soft chest, graying hair, and beleaguered paunch. "Such an old soldier," I say. "Do I actually appeal to you?"

Barrymore frowns at me in the gloom. "Why must you ask such questions?"

Then we are off again, passing a music room where a harpsichord and a fortepiano gather dust. And a two-story library with a winding stair and shelves of fragrant volumes embossed in gold.

"Where exactly are we going?" I ask.

Barrymore squeezes my hand. "A place I sometimes rest when I'm tired from my chores."

A flurry of rooms. Billiard hall. Egyptian gallery. And a little theater with rows of seats facing a wooden stage. On the stage is a copse of leafless trees, trunks all painted white. The sky on the backdrop has a streaked and reddish glow.

I have just enough time to wonder what sort of dramas the Baskervilles might have mounted here. Then Barrymore pulls me into a dark chamber, the walls of which are lined with hunting trophies. He lights a lamp, and taxidermy heads of elk and deer and boar emerge from the shadows. There are more exotic creatures, too, likely from Sir Rodger's fabled time in Africa. A wildebeest. An antelope. A full-bodied crocodile. All of the animals have the same honey-colored glass eyes. And they seem to stare at us as if we are intruders in this, their realm of death.

At the center of the room stands a backless velvet sofa of the sort one might encounter in the lobby of a grand hotel. "Here," Barrymore says. "Come." He pulls me toward the sofa and pushes me down onto the velvet cushion. I immediately unfasten his trousers. His cock strains against the waist of his undergarments. I yank them down to find the fat head of his prick glistening in the lamplight. I am licking him everywhere at once, eager to taste the salt of him. His hard pale thighs. Testicles that hang like river stones. When I slide my tongue up the shaft of his cock to the swollen head, he cries out. And then he is in my mouth, long member pressing at the back of my throat. He grabs a handful of my hair, guiding me. Soon he's pulled me into a standing position, and he has my cock in his mouth. I watch the muscles of his back tense and release, and I glance up only once to see a gazelle staring down at us, passing strange judgment.

Barrymore pauses, pupils dilated, full of candlelight. "Do you want to try something else?"

"What else?" I ask.

He stands and spits into his palm, moving to bend me over the velvet sofa.

"Wait," I say.

He presses his throbbing cock against my flank. "Wait for what?"

"It doesn't work like that for me."

"Doesn't work?"

"It never has. It's painful."

He looks confused but says, "Then be inside of me."

"Are you sure?"

He caresses the edge of my mustache. "Stop asking questions and you'll see." He kneels on the velvet sofa, hiking his ass in the air.

I rub my cock between his cheeks. He moans, catching the tip of my prick with his hole. I push forward, sliding into him. He's all muscle and heat. I lean forward, kissing the space between his shoulder blades, pushing deeper.

He rocks against me, flexing, releasing. A sensation of being milked. And just as I am about to spend, there's a sound in the hall.

I pause my thrusts, shaft still half inside of Barrymore.

Some intruder moves quietly beyond the closed door of the trophy room.

"What is it?" Barrymore asks, face buried in a pillow.

A foot scrapes against the floorboards.

"A step," I whisper. "A dragging step."

"It's him," Barrymore says. "Oh, God. He's come for us."

And only then do I realize that in our haste, we left the hunting rifles in the parlor.

The dragging step comes again. Louder this time. Closer still.

I pull out of Barrymore. He hisses.

The two of us move naked toward the door. I turn the handle softly, opening it only a crack, and we both peer out.

The hall is empty. There is no stranger. No giant from the tower.

"I should check on Sir Henry," I whisper.

Barrymore takes my arm. "Wait."

"But he could be in danger."

"I heard him lock his door earlier," he says. "He's as safe as anyone. And we don't have any weapons. Just stay here, sir. Please." He kisses me, and his mouth is dry. He's frightened. Then he's tugging at my cock, stiffening it once again.

The taxidermy animals with their queer glass eyes watch and listen.

I return with Barrymore to the velvet sofa.

Later, I awake in darkness. The lamp has gone out. The trophy room is silent, cold. As I stare into the shadows before me, an ember of red light appears. There's a crackling sound. A scent of burned tobacco. Someone's smoking a cigarette. I assume it's Barrymore. He spent twice during our encounter. Once in my mouth and a second time onto the shaft of my cock, massaging it with his hand.

I want to touch him again. To feel his lovely warmth.

Still half inside a dream, I reach across the velvet cushion toward the burning ember. I'm about to speak his name when someone strikes a match and lights a small lamp on the end table. The glow of the flame reveals not Barrymore but Beryl Stapleton, face powdered, hair coifed. She's dressed in dark evening clothes, complete with what looks like a fur-lined opera cloak. And she's smoking a rather odd-looking cigarette rolled in black paper.

All the pleasure I received during the night drains out of me, turning into something cold and congealed. "You..." I say.

"A gentleman should offer a more pleasant greeting to a lady, I should think." She taps her cigarette on the edge of a decorative porcelain ashtray. "Manners must be slipping these days in London."

"What are you doing here? Where's Barrymore?"

"Barry—" She puts a finger to her chin, pretending confusion. "Oh, do you mean the servant boy you're inappropriately obsessed with?"

"Where is he?"

"I haven't the foggiest, Dr. Watson. That's not the reason I've come to speak with you."

I sit up and, in horror, realize I'm still naked. Barrymore's seed is dried and crusted on my leg. I hastily pull my trousers from the floor and use them to cover my privates. "Are you a witch, as Henry Baskerville asserts?"

She sighs and takes a drag off her cigarette. "Must we label everything?"

I rub at my face, trying to gather my wits. "You transported me somehow—to London and to the bog."

"Honestly, I just gave you a little nudge. If we need to come up with a category for someone like me, I suppose I'm something of a conservationist. I keep the balance here on the moor."

"The balance of what?"

"Unseen forces," she intones, exhaling a plume of smoke. The scent seems to have intensified. It makes me think of charred earth. A wasteland.

"The Druids have something to do with this, don't they?" I ask, desperately wishing I still had my bottle of laudanum. A mere sip of it would calm my thoughts.

"Druids?" she says. "How imaginative."

"Do not attempt to obscure the truth further. I have work to do. Henry Baskerville and—"

"I assure you everything is fine for now in the House of Baskerville."

"What is it you want?"

She takes a breath. "This is hard to say, honestly. A confession of sorts. I'm having certain difficulties. There's something amiss, you see, and I can't figure out what that something is. It's exceedingly frustrating. And there will be no Sherlock Holmes to help us, isn't that right?"

"Holmes isn't coming," I reply flatly.

"So that leaves me with you. And we need to work quickly before things get out of hand. Or, I suppose I should say, further out of hand."

"Tell me what the Devil you're going on about."

She takes another drag off her cigarette. "Words are imprecise, especially in this matter. I suppose I could show you."

"No!" I raise my hand as if to prevent a blow. I do not want to be transported again.

She smiles. "I thought not. All right. What I need from you is quite simple. You must retrieve Hugo Baskerville's book. The one bound in human skin."

"Human skin?"

"Old Hugo had a flair for the dramatic, I'm afraid. And the morbid. At any rate, you must collect the book and bring it to me at Merripit House. I promise I won't let the butterflies harm you again."

"I've searched for the book. I can't find it."

"Yes, I know. You're not very good at any of this."

"Stop."

"I don't mean to hurt your feelings, Doctor. But you're not. All you do is faun over that boy in various states of intoxication and, from time to time, stumble over dead bodies."

"I am doing the best I can. My life has—"

"Come apart," she says in an almost sympathetic tone. "I'm aware of your history. And now you've been thrust into this." She gestures at the taxidermy heads with her black cigarette. "A primitive carnival. But you must believe me. We have work to do."

"As I've already said, I don't know how to find the book. I can't do what Holmes does."

"Luckily, that's not a requirement. I know where the book is. I just can't retrieve it for some reason."

"Where?"

"The Baskerville stables. In a wicker trunk. There's a filthy old Bible and an empty cup of wine on the lid."

I remember seeing the Bible and the wine cup when I looked for Perkins several days ago. "But the groom told me he had no knowledge of the book's location."

"Perhaps he was lying to you? That never happens in these sorts of affairs, does it?"

"What would a man like Perkins be doing with Hugo Baskerville's grimoire?"

"Following the recipes?" Beryl Stapleton says. "It doesn't matter what he's doing. I must have the book to undo what's been done."

"Someone has summoned the Hound. I saw it."

"It's not a hound. And it hasn't been summoned."

I picture the creature in the mire, swelling and contracting like a lung. Dog that is not a dog. Man that is not a man. "What is it then?"

"Again, words fail me. All I can tell you is that the figure you encountered in the bog is part of the balance. It's necessary."

"It attacked me."

"It most certainly did not. You surprised it. And I dare say the so-called assault was all your doing. Flinging your body into that mud puddle and thrashing all about. What you refer to as the Hound rescued you."

"What?"

"How else do you think you got back to the moor? It dragged you out of the bog. Pulled you to safety and left you there with the sheep."

"The Hound is—"

"Not one of our problems."

I find all of this most difficult to believe. And I suddenly wonder if Beryl Stapleton might be lying. "Do you know who's walking about the house at night? The man with the dragging step? Is he the one committing these murders?"

"I don't have the answer to that question. And that is one of our problems. There are too many elements I cannot see. I believe someone is interfering here. Someone who has gained a certain amount of power, as you say. That's why I need you as my agent."

"And you don't intend to harm anyone?"

She smiles demurely. "I might harm any number of people before this is over. But you needn't worry about that. For now, locate Hugo Baskerville's book and bring it to me."

"Why not ask your brother?"

"Brother?"

"The man who lives with you. The naturalist."

"Oh, he wasn't a naturalist. He was a derelict I found outside Grimpen tavern. His presence was a necessary ruse. It's not proper for a woman to travel without an escort."

"And where is he now?"

She clears her throat. "I'm afraid he has expired. You saw his body or at least the outline of it. It was under that pile of butterflies on the floor of Merripit House."

I picture the mound of dark, fluttering creatures. The sound of their terrible thrumming wings.

Beryl Stapleton sits forward, gazing darkly at me. "Do you agree to help me or not, Dr. Watson?"

I find myself unnerved by her possibilities. If I don't do her bidding, I might end up like the derelict or worse—transported to the bottom of the ocean or the molten center of the earth. "I'll try to find the book, yes."

"Very good. Be quick about it." She snaps her painted fingers.

The room is dark. And once again, I am alone.

## 13

Morning light, the color of milk, streaming through high windows.

I wander ruined halls, searching, at first, for Barrymore. Then for anything I might recognize. But there is only dust and peeling paper. Water-stained silk. Buckling wainscot. As if the house has been abandoned for a hundred years (a thousand years?) Or as if it is not a house at all but rather some crude pretender. A shadow that learned long ago to look like stone and wood and ivy.

*Yet mortar breaks and plaster falls.*

*Illusions are abandoned.*

*Barrymore and Dr. Mortimer, Sir Henry and Perkins the groom. Even Beryl Stapleton herself. Are they all, in fact, a single voice echoing up from an ancient fissure in the earth? Or is it possible I am the lonely voice? The one who trembles and fades. Never a doctor or a soldier. Certainly not a detective. But a dislocated thing. Filled up with so many old and broken desires. Scribbling away in its terrible book.*

I turn a corner in a narrow gaslit hall and hear Holmes's voice inside my head: Poetic rumination, Watson, has never solved a case. Stop distracting yourself. Move toward a solution.

*A solution, yes. Most certainly, Holmes. That is indeed the way forward. I slide my hand along the smooth wallpaper as a question presents itself: what mystery exactly am I solving here? Do I know any longer? Have I ever known?*

I come to a room with vaulted ceilings where a half-finished mural covers one wall. Another queer dream of some long-dead Baskerville, I suppose. Antique jungle. African palms faded to mist. Painted Englishmen lay together in the tall grass, half-naked in the heat. Safari jodhpurs. Velvet cravats. Polished leather riding boots. They talk and drink and sometimes caress one another. A servant carries a tray of ripe fruit and a honey-colored leopard lounges on the low branch of a tree.

*I understand I must leave this room, for no matter my protests. I am the detective now. The only possible detective. But at the same time, I wish I could lose myself here, wander in these painted forests. Far from shadow. Far from mystery. Wouldn't it be lovely to never find my way again?*

*And yet...*

I pass down another gaslit hall. And here, of course, is the marbled foyer. Here, the familiar oaken stair.

*The maze stands triumphant. The pattern has its way.*

*

I climb the stairs to the shadows of the second floor and pause before Sir Henry's room. His door is closed. Hopefully, locked. Yet I dare not try the knob. A mechanical sound issues from within. A creaking of hinges. The wooden mannequin is at its work. There's a moan of pleasure. Sir Henry alive and well. Stuffed full of the ivory phallus. Frigged into strange bliss.

I think again of Barrymore. Naked before me. Young cock in his young hand. "Do you want to try something else?"

I go to my room and splash water on my face. I must be alert, ready for the trials of the day. First to the stables. A search for the lost book. And then to Grimpen Village, the festival with Barrymore. I'll put him on the afternoon train. He'll be safe in London by supper time. At least I'll have done one good thing in all of this.

I sit in my chair, intending to rest there only briefly. But almost as soon as my head touches the velvet backing, I've fallen asleep.

In my dream, the walls of my room open like louvered doors, revealing the African jungle from the half-finished mural. White mist hangs in the trees. Painted birds sing.

The men of the safari are everywhere about, naked now and lithe. Fine cocks, glans the color of hibiscus, drape over-muscled blond thighs. The men talk and laugh. They do not look at me. They do not even seem to recognize my presence. Then something happens to the floor of my room. The carpet and boards begin to shudder. Slowly, they shift and rise, coming together to form a single imposing column. Soon what remains of the walls and ceiling are pulled into the column, too, swelling it, making it strain. The lower floors are drawn in next. The parlor and the gallery. The swimming pool. They all fall together in a great tumescence. Now leaking. Appearing to beckon.

And in the logic of dreams, I realize I must try to fit the entire house, all of Baskerville Hall, inside me.

I move to stand before the great phallus.

The painted men of the forest turn lazily to watch.

I rub the tip of plaster and silk and wood against my fundament. And as I try to open myself, the house presses forward, using all its weight, forcing itself inside.

*I awake, stifling a scream. Shirt soaked with sweat. Cock hard and throbbing.*

Hurriedly, I grab my overcoat and rush down the oaken stair, bursting through the front door and out into the bracingly cold morning. Twisted alder trees greet me. Lonely men against a sunless sky. The air smells of rot and damp. Old October. The end of things.

But despite these grim surroundings, freeing myself from the confines of Baskerville Hall, even for a moment, feels like a blessing.

I raise the collar of my coat against the chill and cross the bleak yard to knock upon the doorframe of the stables. When Perkins does not answer, I step into the sawdust-strewn entryway. There's a warm scent of fresh hay and aged leather. Finally, a place that doesn't feel haunted. I call out the groom's name once and then again. When no answer comes, I approach the wicker trunk where the Bible and empty wine cup rest. They are just as Beryl Stapleton described them. I move both objects, setting them carefully on the floor. Then I lift the lid, expecting to see Hugo Baskerville's ancient yellowed book staring back at me. The face of the many-eyed moon. But the trunk is merely full of riding implements. A crop and bridle. Knotted saddle reigns. I lift them. There's nothing underneath. Either Miss Stapleton was wrong about the location of the book. Or it has been moved. Secreted away.

Behind me then, a thin and wavering voice: "Sir?"

I turn to see Perkins standing in the doorway, looking unsteady. Tufts of white hair. Trembling hands. Somehow, he manages to carry a rather large box of tools.

"Are you searching for something?" he says.

I consider a lie but decide instead to use a tactic Holmes once taught me. Speak the truth when you know it, Watson. Then stand back and watch with care. Villains will often out themselves. "I was looking for Hugo Baskerville's book. Someone told me it would be here."

Perkins squints his watery eyes. "In the stables, sir? The devil book?"

I feel more certain of myself as I speak once more. "That's right. In this very basket."

"There's never been anything in that basket, but what is there now."

I glance again at the pile of riding implements. "Do you mind if I have a look around the rest of the stables?"

"No, sir. Have yourself a good look. But you won't find anything here."

"I'm sure I won't..."

I move deeper into the stables. To my left, a paddock. Shadows of resting horses. And to my right, Perkins's own quarters. I stand at the door of the old man's room, peering inside. A small bed. A basin of water. A wooden cross upon the wall. And something else. A second wicker trunk. Identical in appearance to the one in the entryway. Except there is no Bible or cup of wine. Yet I see the circular red stain of a wine cup. Perhaps this is the trunk Beryl Stapleton meant. I move toward it, making to lift its lid.

"Sir," Perkins's voice once again, harder now, full of warning.

Before I've half turned, something strikes me across the back of the head. There's a flash of light, an explosion of pain. I cry out and fall to my knees. Perkins stands over me, but he's changed. He appears far less frail than he did moments before. There's no curve to his spine or tremor in his hand. It's as if he's somehow stolen strength from the riding horses. He holds, in one clenched fist, a heavy fire iron. "No man in this life," he says through gritted yellow teeth, "should ever... help... a Baskerville." He widens his stance and swings again.

Black curtains fall.

# 14

Somewhere outside my aching head, a slow and heavy footfall.

A dragging step, drawing ever nearer.

I will myself to move. I must escape the malevolent sound. But the pain is too much.

Forcing one eye open, I peer through a red haze to see I am still on the floor of Perkins's room.

The step comes again, echoing. I feel it in every organ of my body. Using all my strength, I manage to pull myself under the bed. I tremble there, head bright with pain. From the low angle, I see only a heavy pair of black boots as they enter the room. I cannot see the face of the man who wears them. One boot takes a step, the other drags behind, hushing across the pinewood. They are old boots. Hobnail. A pointed tow. A low heel. The sort of boots a soldier might have worn in the previous century. The leather is festooned with mold and streaked with dirt.

Now I hear a ragged breath.

The booted figure walks to the center of the room. And though I still cannot see his face, I know it is that of the monstrous stranger from the tower. The giant with eyes like spider's eggs and a swollen hanging tongue. He's looking for me. Listening.

I hold my breath. I do not move. Blood trickles down into my eye from whatever wound Perkins opened in my skull.

Then there's something like a voice. The most terrible I have ever heard. Low and crawling. The baritone of a man who might have once commanded armies. But now, he speaks a garbled noise as if he remembers how to use his throat but doesn't have the sense for words.

The voice seems to ask a question of the silence. Where are you, old thing? Crawling thing? We are not so different, you and I. Come let me break your bones.

When there is no answer, the boots turn and slowly move off.

I remain under the bed, shaking.

How long do I wait there in the dust?

I cannot say exactly, for fear changes time.

And I am so afraid the mad stranger will return. That he will have me, destroy me as he destroyed the birds in the southern tower. As he likely destroyed Charles Baskerville and the convict called Seldon and Lord V of Laughter Hall. I think of his rotting boots. Dead leather boots. The drag of his step.

*Have I solved a mystery here? Is this what it feels like?*

*No. Certainly not.*

*To provide a solution is to restore order. To make the world clean. As Holmes makes the world clean. All I have done is to further widen an already ragged hole. A rip in the shroud. For what does any of this mean? Perkins the groom? The yellow book?*

*The stranger with the dragging step? No man in this life should ever help a Baskerville.*

I force myself to slide out from under the bed, knowing I must be strong. I have work to do. Barrymore is in danger. And Sir Henry too. I am here to protect these men.

I hurry back to Baskerville Hall, throwing open the door and calling out.

Dr. Mortimer appears at the top of the oaken stair. He's dressed in a well-made traveling suit, carrying a steaming cup of tea. "Dr. Watson?" he says, descending three steps. "Good lord. Your head!"

I reach up and feel the tacky blood on my scalp. There's still some pain, but thankfully, it has abated slightly. "My head will be fine."

"But what happened to you?"

"Perkins," I say.

"Perkins?"

"He attacked me."

Dr. Mortimer raises his manicured brow. "Why would old Perkins attack anyone?"

"I'm going to Grimpen Village to get the constable. I'll take Barrymore with me in case I need assistance. Keep watch over Sir Henry. Lock all the doors. And if you see Perkins or a very large man who walks with a dragging step, you must flee. They both pose the gravest of dangers to this house."

"Dr. Watson, this is all quite astonishing."

"We have no more time for talk, Dr. Mortimer. Do you understand me?"

"I do, but—"

I make my way to the back of the house, toward the glass doors leading onto the Yew Alley. Barrymore is emerging from his quarters, hair combed and cleanly parted, white shirt pressed, ready for a day of work. "Grab a change of clothes," I say. "We're leaving now."

"Your head," he says.

"Never mind about my head. There's something going on here I do not fully understand. But I believe it's going to get much worse before it gets better."

Barrymore already has a duffle packed. He grabs it, and we hurry out onto the moorland road. I look everywhere about as we walk. But there's no sign of Perkins or the towering stranger.

"What happened to you, sir?" Barrymore says.

"Stop calling me 'sir.'" I glance behind us again to make sure we are not followed. A wind blows down from the highlands, rustling the yellow asphodel. "You don't need to know anything more about what's going on here, Barrymore. In fact, it's better if you forget all of it. You'll have a new life in London. I'll visit you if you like."

A howl rises on the moor. I cannot say if it's the wind or …

"The Hound of the Baskervilles," Barrymore whispers.

I attempt to ignore his statement, refusing to allow myself even the briefest twinge of fear. There's no point in thinking about the Hound. It is not, as Beryl Stapleton says, one of our problems.

I focus instead on Barrymore himself. He looks remarkable

in the rays of the afternoon sun. The sort of young man who is not merely handsome but rather defines handsomeness. And I want to kiss him again. No matter the pain in my head. No matter the dangers of the moor.

But I do not pause. I force myself to walk on. I must get him to safety.

When we arrive in Grimpen village, the Harvest Festival is already underway. Narrow lanes are strung with autumn garland. Dried apple and crowberry. Marigold and guelder rose. Gourds, all red and orange, carved with grinning faces, leer up at us from every doorstep. And a great bonfire burns in the town square, filling the streets with aromatic smoke.

I watch as a bearded man in a gray cloak circles the fire, weaving between the Roman swords. He holds a curved sickle above his head. Veiled women carry baskets of turnips and dark fruit, singing softly.

None of this odd pageantry holds my attention for long, for there is something more unusual still that waits on a roughhewn platform before the ancient tavern on the square. It is an effigy made of nettle and straw and hairgrass, taller than a man, and in the shape of a great looming hound. Someone has placed two white stones in the creature's grassy head to represent eyes. And the hound appears to keep vigil, watching in silence over the men and women of Grimpen. Offerings have been laid at the animal's feet. Sheaves of wheat and silver coins. Horseshoes and ragdolls. There's even a set of wooden teeth.

"They worship it?" I whisper to Barrymore.

"And fear it too," he replies.

I take his arm. Nothing about this place feels safe.

We make our way to the post office. The bell above the door rings as we enter, and the postmaster looks up, peering at us from behind the polished glass of his spectacles.

"One ticket to London," I say. "Euston Station."

The postmaster stares at the wound in my head with some concern. "Do you need medical assistance, Dr. Watson?"

"I do not. Just the ticket, please."

"I hope you'll stay to observe our celebration, at least for a short while."

"The ticket is for my young friend."

"Well," the postmaster says, checking the wall clock. "You're just in time for the afternoon train from London. We should hear it any—"

A high whistle sounds in the distance.

I glance at Barrymore. He's pale with excitement, likely unable to believe he is leaving Dartmoor. And I am so happy to offer this chance to him.

The postmaster hands me a yellow ticket.

We step outside, and Barrymore moves immediately toward the platform. But I take his arm and point to a nearby alley. "This way first."

He follows me, and we stand facing each other.

I rub my throbbing head, trying to decide exactly what to say. "I want to tell you... I suppose I want to say thank you."

A crease forms on his fine brow. "What are you thanking me for?"

"I have known men. All my life, I have known them. I was

with one man for some twenty years. He was unkind. Not at first, you understand, but as time wore on. He grew tired of me, I think. And time is not what I believed it to be. It moves so very quickly." I pause, searching for the right words. "I barely thought I'd be able to catch hold of you as we flew by one another. But it was good, you know, to meet you. Good to be with you. Even if only for a short while. This is such an odd place. And you are so very much alive, beautiful really, like the men I used to know, and well—"

The London train shrieks into Grimpen Station, filling the alley with steam. A conductor calls out, "Make way. Make way. Gentleman coming in from London! Deboarding passenger!"

"Everything I say now will sound foolish," I continue. "It will likely mean nothing to you in the end. You might not even remember it in a few years."

"That isn't true." Barrymore takes my hand. I feel the callouses on his palm. I look into his eyes, and because there is no time for anything else, I lean forward and kiss him.

When Barrymore puts his strong arms around me, it feels like everything that time has stolen is suddenly returned.

And then, from the smoke at the head of the alley, a sharp voice. Commanding. Decisive. Perhaps even slightly amused. "My dear Watson, what on earth are you up to now?"

At first, I hope the voice might merely be inside my muddled, throbbing head. But I turn to look, and there in the field of gray smoke: an Inverness cape and a deerstalker cap. A shining black walking stick.

Mr. Sherlock Holmes. Tall and lean and highbrowed. Sharp beak of a nose. And gray eyes that are sharper still.

He was the gentleman who arrived on the afternoon train.

"Holmes," I say, feeling something like horror in my gut. "But—"

"You didn't think I was going to come, did you, Watson? I can tell from the look on your face." He is amused. "And I see you've found love in Devonshire, with..." he glances at Barrymore, "an urchin?"

I stumble, trying to get words out. "This is the Baskerville's servant. He's a good young man, Holmes. I'm putting him on a train to London to protect him."

Holmes looks rather surprised at this. "Putting him on a train? Why, if you do that, you'll be freeing the very criminal we've been searching for. The culprit of these many crimes."

"Culprit?" I look at Barrymore, knowing Holmes cannot be correct. Yet has there ever been a time when Holmes was not correct?

Barrymore's body stiffens. He's paler than ever now and looks something like an animal caught in a trap. Before I know what's happening, he's running toward the head of the alley.

Holmes raises an arm to grab the boy. Barrymore ducks under it. But I realize the raised arm was only a distraction. For Holmes has stuck out the tip of his walking stick, tripping Barrymore, causing him to fall flat on his face in the dust. In a single precise motion, Holmes grabs him by the shock of his hair and pulls him to a standing position, simultaneously twisting the boy's arm behind him and pinning it so he cannot move.

"There we are," Holmes says brightly. "Now then, a carriage waits for us in the street. Let's go have a look at this Baskerville Hall, shall we?"

# 15

"Holmes, wait," I say.

But the Great Detective does not wait. He moves instead with cold purpose, pushing a stumbling Barrymore down the alley, tartan cape fluttering in the breeze.

The word he spoke, culprit, still hangs in the smoke-ridden air.

But Barrymore cannot be any sort of culprit. Beautiful boy. Restoration of all that is lost. Surely, he cannot.

I hurry after them. And as we pass the festival on the village green, the men in gray robes and veiled women turn to look. Even the postmaster leans in his doorway, arms folded, silently watching from behind shining spectacles.

I've encountered the effects of Holmes's celebrity before. Citizens of London often pause to observe his movements, attempting to guess the details of his next remarkable case. A number have even approached him to sign copies of The Strand. But the attention from these villagers feels altogether different. Their gaze, so utterly solemn, as if they attend a funeral parade.

I glance toward the looming tavern on the square. The effigy of the great hound appears to watch us too. Jaw hanging. Eyes white. An expression of occult contemplation.

"We are making quite the scene," I say to Holmes. "You can release Barrymore. He won't run again."

Without pausing or even deigning to glance in my direction, Holmes says, "I'm sure you'll understand, Watson, if I do not accept your assessment of the current situation."

This dismissal is not surprising, of course. In Holmes's view, I have long been Watson the fool. Watson the eye that does not see. Yet, in this instance, I am prompted to stop in the middle of Grimpen thoroughfare.

Festival garlands rustle around us. The grinning gourds seem almost on the verge of laughter.

It is true I have been the fool. I've played that part for far too long. But I have never, in my estimation, been the eye that does not see.

I see everything, in fact. And I feel it too. Depths of sorrow. Caverns of pain.

And this case—our "current situation"—is something new. Because for once, I am quite certain it does not belong entirely to him.

"Holmes," I say loudly enough for the robed men and women of Grimpen to hear. "You are making a significant mistake."

He stops abruptly at this, shoulders tensed. Then slowly, he turns to face me with Barrymore still in his grip. His gaze is like a lamp, and I am fixed in its awful beam. "A mistake?" he says, voice silken. "And why exactly do you think that, Watson?"

"There's a great deal I haven't told you."

"Is there?"

"Yes. Details I didn't include in my letters."

Holmes's nostrils flare almost imperceptibly. I recognize this as one of the expressions he normally reserves for murderers and blackmailers. "What is most surprising to me and most irritating, I suppose, is that you somehow believe I am unable to read between your lines."

"But there are entire episodes missing," I say. "Facts left out."

He smiles thinly. "Well then, I suppose we'll just have to wait and see, won't we?" He jerks Barrymore about and pushes the boy forward once again.

The carriage Holmes hired to return us to Baskerville Hall is not some meager wagonette but a finely burnished coach. Cherrywood panels inlaid with ivory. Brass lamps all aglow. I have no idea how he managed to secure such a grand conveyance anywhere near rustic Grimpen Village. But despite its fine appearance, I understand its purpose well enough. This is a prison wagon, and Barrymore and I are to be its unwilling wards.

The driver, a gaunt gentleman dressed in a black frockcoat, opens the passenger door, and Holmes puts Barrymore inside. He and I take our seats on the bench opposite.

Barrymore stares down at his hands, ruffled hair hanging low over his brow.

I lean toward him. "I'm sorry about all this. We'll get it sorted out when we arrive at the house. I promise you."

He does not look up at the sound of my words. There's not even the twitch of a finger or shift of a boot. He behaves, in all honesty, like one who has committed a crime.

"Holmes," I say, "I really must insist you tell me what's going on here."

The Great Detective parts the carriage curtain to look out at the still watchful villagers on the green. "As you well know," he says, "that is not my method. I have a few more facts to gather when we reach the house, and then I'll lay the whole thing out. For now, I must conserve my energies."

"But, Holmes—"

He clears his throat and leans back against the velvet seat cushion, pulling the deerstalker down over his eyes.

*The carriage jounces along the rutted moorland road, and I continue to gaze at Barrymore, wishing I could take his hand and give him comfort. But there is no comfort to be had for either of us. There is only one confusion laid upon the next.*

It appears word of Holmes's arrival has already reached Baskerville Hall, for Dr. Mortimer waits in visible anticipation on the portico of the house.

The carriage slows, and when we finally come to a stop, Holmes reanimates, springing forth to take the doctor's hand.

"It is so good of you to come, Mr. Holmes," Dr. Mortimer says. "Everything has been so difficult for us here these last few days." He glances at me as he says this as if to imply I am the reason for these difficulties.

"Very good to meet you, Dr. Mortimer," Holmes says. "I presume there is a secure room where we might hold onto young Mr. Barrymore for a time. Something on the second floor, perhaps. A space with no windows so he can't signal to anyone."

"Signal?" Dr. Mortimer looks vaguely confused for a moment but then says, "Well, yes, I think I could find something suitable."

Holmes turns his gaze on me once more. "Watson, I'd like you to go and fetch the Stapleton woman. She'll be at her cottage on the moor." He checks his pocket watch. "We'll reconvene in the parlor at six o'clock sharp." Then to Dr. Mortimer again: "If Sir Henry Baskerville could be present for our meeting as well, that would be most beneficial."

"Of course. I'll alert the baronet."

"Very good," Holmes says. "Everyone to his task." And with that, he disappears into the shadows of the foyer, followed quickly by Dr. Mortimer grasping Barrymore's arm.

I turn to look at the stables. They're silent now.

No sign of Perkins or the stranger with the dragging step.

No sign of anything at all.

And I am left like some errand boy or, worse yet, an afterthought. I make my way quietly down the stairs from the portico and onto the bleak and barren road.

When I am halfway to Merripit House, I find I cannot continue. My limbs are heavy. And the splitting pain in my head from the blows of Perkins's fire iron has returned.

I sit on a large rock amongst a fall of yellow leaves and listen to the wind on the moor. There is no distant howling now. No hint of strange fantasy. There's only desolation here. Blasted earth and the ever-darkening sky. I watch a carrion crow peck at an outgrowth of prickling gorse.

Then for reasons I do not understand, I put my face in my hands. My cheeks, I find, are damp. Not from the mist on the moor, but because I am crying. And as soon as I realize this, the crying becomes something greater still. Shoulders rise and fall with hitching breath.

I rub at my eyes and press my fingers against my lips, trying to stop this outpouring.

Yet I cannot stop.

I ask myself why an old man from London would be sitting on a rock in the middle of a country he does not know, weeping like a fool. I wept, of course, when Holmes put an end to our relationship. And I wept again after I said goodbye to dear Mrs. Hudson on Baker Street. But all of that had been my life for some twenty years. And now I weep for what? For my own grotesque ineptitude? Can it be true Barrymore has been deceiving me all this while? Have I gained nothing from my years of devotion to such a cold intelligence as Holmes? No modicum of insight?

To comfort myself, I run my fingers through my graying mustache, a gesture from my younger days. I used to rub at the newly sprouted bristles above my lip as I held forth on some topic to entertain the soldiers of the Fifth Northumberland. I'd pretend to think deeply, pretentiously, as if I was some philosopher or self-important don. The men had laughed. And I had laughed. And we had all been filled with such good cheer.

Perhaps I weep now because, for the briefest of moments, a future had seemed possible. Barrymore and I rambling the streets of London. Dark figures in a cozy fog. We'd take in a comedy at the Royal Albert and stop by Simpson's for a late-night supper. It would not matter if some passerby mistook us for father and son, for we would be such friendly companions that the whole world, with all its ugliness and disdain, would be blotted out. I'd take Barrymore home with me, and we'd tuck ourselves into bed, still laughing, holding onto one another.

But such things as this will never come.

For not only is the past a ruin, the future is in tatters too.

"Dr. Watson?" A voice on the moor. One I know all too well. I remove my hands from my face and open my eyes. Beryl Stapleton stands over me in a pale dress like those worn by the weird fairy women I observed near the megalith. Her dark hair falls loosely around her shoulders. She is oddly radiant in the light. Something about her at this moment reminds me of my own mother. How she used to look down at me as I lay crying on the floor. Stand up, John, she'd say. Nothing is as bad as all that.

But Beryl Stapleton is not like my mother. She is, in fact, not like anyone's mother. Instead, she is the sort of thing that would have been spoken of in hushed tones in a previous age. Old women might have made hexes to ward her off.

"Are you crying?" she says.

I clear my throat. "It would appear so, Miss Stapleton."

She looks vaguely uncomfortable. "Well..." She pulls a folded handkerchief from the bodice of her dress. "Here. Take this."

I gaze at the handkerchief, perhaps expecting it to transform into an adder and leap at my face. But it proves instead to be an entirely conventional piece of linen.

"Don't just stare at it, Doctor," she says. "Dry yourself."

I follow her instructions, wiping my eyes.

"Did you find the book?"

"No," I mutter. "It was not where you said it would be."

"Of course, it was. I don't make mistakes about things like that."

I shake my head. "It seems you have done so in this case. But you'll be pleased to know Sherlock Holmes has arrived."

"Sherlock Holmes?" she says. And I'm glad to see I've startled her. "You said he wasn't coming."

"He arrived on the afternoon train."

"And your head?"

"Perkins. He hit me with a fire iron."

"Did he say why?"

"He said, 'No man in this life should ever help a Baskerville.'"

She looks further perplexed. "And yet he has spent his entire life helping Baskervilles."

I touch the painful edge of my headwound. "Maybe it only appears so. And there's another man. A giant with a dragging step."

"This is all becoming far too convoluted. And frankly, I don't care about any of it. I only want the book."

"Holmes will find it. He'll solve everything as he always does. He's taken Barrymore into a kind of custody."

"Your servant boy?"

I nod.

She takes a deep breath. "We really should be going."

I stand from the rock, and it is as we turn toward Baskerville Hall that I see a great column of black smoke rising against the bleak sky. "Dear God," I say. "The house is on fire."

"I apologize for this," she says, raising her hand and snapping her fingers. The moor spins madly, and we are suddenly standing in the yard of Baskerville Hall. I must wait for the nauseating vertigo to pass in order to realize it's not the main house that's burning but the stables. The horses have been led some distance away, and Dr. Mortimer watches as men, perhaps servants from a nearby house, toss buckets of water upon the blaze.

"What's happened, Dr. Mortimer?" Beryl Stapleton asks.

He turns sharply. "Miss Stapleton. Dr. Watson. I didn't hear your approach."

"The fire," she prompts.

"I haven't the faintest idea. I was upstairs tending to Sir Henry when I smelled smoke. And now this."

"Perkins did it," I say. "Likely to conceal some kind of evidence. Where is Holmes?"

Dr. Mortimer glances over his shoulder. "He's somewhere inside the house. I called for him, but he did not come."

The imposing granite facade of Baskerville Hall shimmers in the smoke. "I'll find him," I say. I lower my head and walk toward the stone steps, ready to bring all of this to a close.

# 16

Smoke from the stable fire has crept into the foyer of Baskerville Hall, bringing with it a haze and a scent of scorched cedar. There is some other difference too. The soul of the house (if a house can be said to have a soul) seems unquiet. Perhaps the presence of Sherlock Holmes has made it so. He wanders somewhere, observing secrets, prying at that which does not want to be seen. Or maybe there is some other form of disturbance. Perkins and the stranger with the dragging step, lurking just out of sight, plotting further horrors.

Whatever the case, the manor seems troubled, as I am troubled.

"Hello?" an anxious voice calls from the landing.

I look up to see a pallid Henry Baskerville, still in his nightdress, gripping the polished handrail as if frightened of falling down the stairs.

"Is my house on fire, Dr. Watson? Dr. Mortimer said he would return with a report, but he has not done so."

"It's not the house, Sir Henry," I say in what I hope is a reassuring tone. "It's the stables."

"The stables!" He acts as if this is somehow worse news. "But what of the horses? And Perkins?"

"The horses have been rescued. And Perkins—" I do not know what to say about the old groom. Should I tell Sir Henry he attacked me? Would there be any point in that? I decide against such a revelation. "I'm looking for Sherlock Holmes."

"Dr. Mortimer told me he's arrived," Sir Henry says. "He's going to put all of this right, isn't he?"

"I'm quite sure he will, yes. But have you seen him?"

Sir Henry looks over one shoulder and then the other as if Holmes might spontaneously manifest. "No. But I should very much like to."

"He's asked us to gather in the parlor at six."

"And he will explain what happened to my poor Charlie?"

"Most certainly. But for now, I must continue my search."

"Very good," Sir Henry says. "I'll wait for further news about the fire."

I nod and move off toward the central hall.

Dining room and billiards room and silent little theater.

I call out for Holmes but hear nothing in response. Soon I find myself in the portrait gallery. This room, too, is tinged with smoke. Long-dead Baskervilles observe me through a violet haze. Here is Sir Rodger in a gaberdine suit, brandishing an elephant gun. And here, his mother, Old Madam, narrow-chinned and hollow-eyed, clutching her silver cane. Two pale children stand arm-in-arm by a milk-white brook, very likely Sir Charles and Sir Henry in their youth. And lording over them all in his vast gilded frame—Hugo Baskerville. Flesh the color of curdled milk. Eyes shining. A fall of blackish curls. He wears the red coat of a Royalist general and the countenance of a depraved sorcerer. In one hand, he holds his grimoire embossed with the many-eyed moon, and in the other, a gleaming broadsword. I look down the length of him, the layers of velvet and lace. And when I arrive at his boots, I stop. For they are hobnail boots. A pointed toe and a low heel. The same as those of the stranger who entered the stable, searching for me. The man with the dragging step. Dead leather boots. I look again at Hugo Baskerville's glowering face and picture his tongue extended, eyes bulging. I turn away from the portrait, knowing I must find Holmes. For he will make sense of this. He will restore reason to this most unreasonable place.

As I pass once more into the dim-lit hall, I hear a voice coming from above. "Dr. Watson..." I look up, confused. A large brass grate of the sort meant to allow air to circulate between the first and second floors is mounted in the hall ceiling. Barrymore himself peers down through its bars. This passageway must be located directly beneath the room in which he is imprisoned.

"Are you all right?" I ask. The very sight of him makes me feel relieved.

"It doesn't matter." He speaks softly, as if not wanting to be overheard.

"Of course, it matters. I'll come and get you out of there."

"No."

"Why not?"

"Because I belong here," he says.

"Belong? Barrymore, tell me what you've done. It can't be all that—"

"I didn't mean to cause you so much strife. When you offered me passage to London, I should have refused. But the idea of escape... it was so tempting."

"I don't understand. Did you have something to do with the death of Charles Baskerville? Or, for that matter, Seldon the convict and Lord V of Laughter Hall?"

He is silent for so long I begin to think I should repeat my question. But finally, he says, "I am the means. If not the cause."

"The means?"

"Without me, my uncle wouldn't have been able to carry out his plans."

"Your uncle?"

"Granduncle, to be exact."

"And who is that?"

He hesitates as if deciding whether or not to answer. "Perkins," he says finally.

This revelation is as startling to me as any I have ever heard from even Sherlock Holmes. "But your surname."

"My father was called Barrymore. My mother was a Perkins. She went mad as so many of them do. It's the fault of old Hugo... his legacy."

"The boys of the village," I say, thinking of the youths Hugo Baskerville dragged from the streets of Grimpen. Those he forced to watch his dark dealings. The Hound opening him like a fissure in the earth.

"His rites have haunted my family for generations," Barrymore says. "Many of the families in Grimpen bear the same scar. My own mother ran away, never to be seen again. Her father hanged himself. And his father before that drowned one of his children in the bog. What Hugo Baskerville revealed to us... it cannot be forgotten."

"What exactly did he reveal?"

"I will not tell you, Dr. Watson. Thank God I do not even know all of it. For to learn the secrets in full is to be changed. My uncle is set to punish the Baskervilles for these revelations."

"Punish them how?"

"By stamping out the family line, all that remains."

"But what have you to do with any of this?"

"He is too old and infirm for such dealings as were necessary."

"What dealings, Barrymore?"

"With the Hound." He gently touches the bars of the brass grate. "The creature is not what anyone believes. Not a monster. Not some specter. It, too, is a lonely thing, cursed to wander the mire. And it requires certain... companionship."

"You acted as its companion?"

"Yes, sir. And because of that, it has made agreements."

"What are these agreements?"

"My uncle will find me and murder me if I say. I only wanted to tell you, sir—Dr. Watson—that you must leave this house. You and your friend Mr. Holmes. You must both return to London where you'll be safe. For there is no way to stop what has already begun. No way at all."

"Barrymore, Holmes has solved many an unsolvable case. And he will do the same here. Then I will set you free. This isn't your fault. I'm quite sure you only did what your uncle asked of you."

He leans closer. "I implored him not to hurt Sir Henry. The baronet is not a villain. But my uncle will not listen."

"I'll find Holmes. He'll bring all of this to a sensible close."

Barrymore threads his fingers through the grate.

"I'll come for you soon. I promise."

After moving through what seems like countless darkened rooms, I finally discover Holmes standing alone in Barrymore's dim and drafty quarters.

He doesn't look up when I pause in the doorway. He's holding something, studying it with care.

As I gaze at my old friend, I find myself suddenly and inexplicably disconcerted. Not because his presence threatens me. The initial shock of seeing him at Grimpen Station has passed. I am more than familiar with his interest in the element of surprise. Instead, I am uneasy because it feels as if something is wrong with the scene's very fabric. A feature I cannot quite name.

Holmes's profile is just as it should be, of course. The high pale brow and aquiline nose. Thin lips I have kissed, time and again.

I recognize the intensity of his concentration too. He's weighing some significant detail, moving toward a clever solution.

But at the same time, something feels entirely amiss.

Perhaps some part of me realizes he does not belong in these strange environs. Nor do I, for that matter. Barrymore was correct about that.

Holmes and I should be in London right now, enjoying a snifter of brandy in the warming glow of 221B.

This thought causes my heart to turn back for the briefest of moments.

I remember all that I loved about my old friend.

And the safety of that love.

Holmes shifts, and the light from the hall reveals what he holds. At first think it must be one of Barrymore's volumes—London for a Day: Scenes of the City or physical exercises for athletes. But then I recognize the sickly yellow hue of its binding. The pages rotted through with age.

"My God." I step into the room. "You found it."

Holmes glances up at me, and there is such an odd expression on his narrow face. Is it fear, I wonder? Or something more improbable—doubt. "What exactly is this, Watson?" he says.

"It's Hugo Baskerville's book. The one Perkins told me—"

"I know it's his book. But what is the meaning of the writing within?"

"May I see?" I move to look at the handwritten pages. But before I can read even a single line, Holmes snaps the volume shut. He touches the odd embossment of the many-eyed moon raised in the cured leather. I am reminded of Beryl Stapleton's words: the book is bound in human skin.

"The moon," Holmes says. "An astrological reference. A symbol of the unconscious mind. Meaningless, of course, and yet..."

"What does the book say? You must tell me. I've been searching for it."

"It was here all along," Holmes replies distractedly. "The servant kept it under his bed. Likely hiding it from the old groom."

"Hiding it?"

"Your young friend believes Mr. Perkins has taken this affair a step too far. And in that assessment at least, he's undoubtedly correct." Holmes tucks the book under his arm and walks out of the room, moving purposefully down the narrow servant's hall. I follow and watch as he opens the leaded glass doors of the Yew Alley and steps out into the brisk October air. "This is where Sir Charles's body was found?" he asks after I've joined him on the gravel walkway.

"That's right. And the convict I wrote to you about: Seldon. He was discovered here too."

Holmes gazes at the crooked yew trees as if their branches hold some obscure meaning. "And there were footprints?"

"According to Dr. Mortimer, yes. The footprints of an enormous hound."

He walks along the Yew Alley as if tracing someone's path, steps neither I nor anyone else would be able to see. He kneels to examine something in the dirt. "What time is it, Watson?"

I take out my pocket watch. "Nearly 5:30."

"Go to the parlor," he says. "Make sure everyone is gathered. Ask Dr. Mortimer to retrieve the servant boy as well. I'll explain everything soon."

"Of course." I move toward the leaded glass doors, but before passing through them, I turn back, realizing it's entirely possible I won't find another moment alone with Holmes, not for a long while at least. "This may not be the best time for questions," I say.

"It most certainly isn't," he replies, scraping at the dirt.

"It's important though, I'm afraid. Something that's been weighing quite heavily upon me."

"Spit it out then."

"Well, Holmes, if I were to return to London—to Baker Street—after all of this is through, would you still be there?"

"At Baker Street?"

"Yes."

"Where else would I be, Watson?" He glances at me in mild annoyance. "Is there some other less obvious question you're trying to ask?"

"I'm finding it difficult to put into words."

He studies the gray dirt that coats his index finger. "Then perhaps you shouldn't do so."

"No. I must try. I suppose I want to ask, will I be there?" I realize how strange this question sounds the moment I speak it out loud, but I also understand I cannot take it back. And it is, in fact, as close to the question I'd been wanting to ask as I can possibly come.

"Where?" Holmes says.

"At Baker Street."

"Do you mean to ask if you'll find yourself there—as if you're split in two? Are you feeling well, Watson?"

"No. I'm afraid I haven't felt like myself since I arrived at this place. I'm sorry."

Holmes blinks as if there's dust in his eyes. "I actually had a dream you returned to Baker Street. You stood in the parlor and spoke to me. I don't remember exactly what you said."

"No?"

He tilts his head as if searching for some detail. "Perhaps you'll open your medical practice again when you come back to London. You can have a cozy little storefront just down the street."

"I don't think so, Holmes. I'm too far behind the times for that."

"Well, I'm sure you'll find some way forward. You've always been industrious enough when necessary."

"I suppose that's right, isn't it?"

"It is indeed. I know you well."

I turn toward the leaded glass doors.

"Watson," Holmes says.

I look back at him.

He's peering at me with his curious gray eyes. When he speaks, there is at least something of my old companion in his tone, the man I met so many years ago through our mutual acquaintance, Stamford. "This will only last a little while. And then you'll find your footing again. It's not as though you'll be lost forever, my dear."

I nod, attempting composure. "I'm sure that's the case."

## 17

Perhaps it's because I am busy telling myself I'm not a fool, that I have not wasted my life wandering the passages of some desperate illusion alongside Sherlock Holmes. Or perhaps it's because I'm thinking of Barrymore and Henry Baskerville, how I meant to save them but could not. How I've never been able to save anyone. Not even myself. Whatever the reason, I make one wrong turn after the next on my way to the parlor, and soon I arrive at an unfamiliar part of the house.

*It's not as though you'll be lost forever, my dear.*

*(He didn't say "my dear Watson," a phrase that has become mere formality between us. How many times have I written it? He said only, "my dear." When did he last speak those simple words to me? How many years has it been?)*

In the unfamiliar wing of the house, I pause before a closed door that bears a brass plaque with an odd inscription: Preserved within are the remains of the original Baskerville farmhouse that occupied this land until Robert Baskerville, Knight of Erdisley, broke ground for the Great House in 1487.

I realize I should find my way to the parlor. I have a job to do. But curiosity gets the best of me.

I turn the dust-covered knob, expecting to find some kind of museum within. However, when the door swings open, something far more fantastical is revealed.

I am looking out upon what appears to be a vista, the low rocky plain of the moor sprawling beneath a painted sky. The color of the sky is brighter and bluer than any I have seen over leaden Devonshire. And there in the distance is a humble stone house of the sort one might have found in England before the Tudors reigned.

It seems quite unbelievable that such a landscape could exist inside a house. And yet here it is.

I step carefully over the threshold and walk along a stony path toward the crumbling farmstead, frequently glancing over my shoulder to ensure the door through which I entered remains.

Of course, the door is a blemish on the otherwise pristine horizon.

The farmhouse itself is much closer than it first appeared. Some illusion of perspective, I suppose. When I reach it, I peer through the rounded windows at a little wooden table, a cheerful hearth, and the semblance of a sitting room.

I can almost hear the soft murmur of voices.

A quiet clink of dishes.

I wonder what sort of Baskervilles might have lived in this place before the endless corridors and dark chambers bloomed.

Before the Hound and old Hugo.

I wonder how different these people's lives might have been.

And who exactly preserved this cottage? Was it some goodhearted ancestor? A man or woman who wanted to leave a reminder that once there was morning and evening and work to be done?

I touch the worn planks of the rustic door, almost daring to open it. But at the last instant, I pull my hand away.

Breaking such a seal, letting the present moment in, would be a terrible mistake.

For now, more than ever, I understand time makes things so strange.

Men and places.

I turn to look out over the painted moor.

Impossibly, a cold wind has begun to blow.

# 18

By the time I locate the parlor, everyone but Holmes himself is already gathered there. They form an uncomfortable rogues' gallery, poised and waiting in the gaslight. Beryl Stapleton sits by the low fire, ankles crossed. She's dressed in satin evening clothes and holds one of her black cigarettes between two fingers. Dr. Mortimer stands stiffly near a seated Barrymore, who gazes up at me with shrinking fear. And then there is Sir Henry himself, scion of the house, pale and agitated but finally free of his nightshirt. He's dressed in a tweed suit and silk neckerchief monogrammed with the Baskerville coat of arms.

"Where is Mr. Holmes?" Sir Henry asks anxiously.

I check my watch. It's nearly six o'clock. "We've only a short while to wait, I should think. Holmes is prompt. Unless he has reason not to be."

"Does he have the book?" Beryl Stapleton asks.

"He does."

"No!" Barrymore makes to stand from his chair, but Dr. Mortimer places a firm hand on the boy's shoulder and presses him back into the seat.

"And Mr. Holmes has answers for us as well?" Sir Henry says. "Does he know who murdered my poor Charlie?"

"Holmes will have answers, yes," I reply. "I'm quite certain of that."

Then a shout comes from the corridor. I recognize the rasping voice as that of Perkins. "Let go of me, I say! You'll wish you had not done this, Mr. Sherlock Holmes."

"On the contrary," Holmes says cheerfully. "As you may know, solving mysteries is a bit of a hobby of mine."

The two of them appear in the shadows of the parlor door, Holmes leveling a revolver at the old groom. Holmes still has the jaundiced book tucked firmly beneath his arm.

"Where did you find him?" I ask, quite astonished.

"All in good time, Watson." Holmes gestures toward a chair with the barrel of the revolver. "If you'll take a seat, Mr. Perkins."

"I will not!"

Holmes calmly pulls the hammer back.

Perkins glares at the weapon. "You will be punished," he growls. "And punished severely." He makes his way to a seat far from the others.

Holmes stands in the doorway, surveying us. "Thank you all for coming. This has been, I believe, one of my most difficult cases to date. Wouldn't you agree, Watson?"

I nod, though I think I would use a far stronger word than "difficult."

"It's been particularly vexing, as you all well know," Holmes continues, "because there is a significant amount of spiritualist falderal mixed into the narrative. Stories of witches and Druids and spectral hounds." He glances at Beryl Stapleton, who smiles faintly and takes a drag off her cigarette. "A rational mind recognizes all of it as useless bric-a-brac, of course."

"Useless, is it?" Perkins mutters from his chair.

Holmes ignores him. "I will now demonstrate that I've managed to pull the facts from the proverbial mire."

"Oh, Mr. Holmes," Sir Henry says. "Thank you, sir. Thank you for rescuing my house."

"Always happy to serve," Holmes says. "And we must also thank my trusted friend Dr. Watson for his work here. The two letters he wrote provided enough information that I'd nearly solved the case before I even set foot in this house."

"Holmes!" I say, confused. "I know exactly what I put in those letters, and there was nothing of a solution there. Why it was barely even a beginning."

"Not so. You provided what was perhaps the most significant fact right up front."

"And what was that?" I recognize we are falling into the rhythm of our old banter, the routine of a parlor trick. Yet I cannot help myself. There is comfort in it, and I must admit I am more than interested in knowing what answers he has found.

"In your first letter, you mentioned Sir Charles Baskerville was in the Yew Alley well after midnight on the evening of his death," Holmes says. "And I immediately thought: whyever would the scion of a great house go out walking at such an hour?"

"You're right to ask such a question, Mr. Holmes," Sir Henry says. "I never knew my cousin to go walking like that. He always slept far better than I."

Holmes nods. "One reason a man might do so, of course, is if he'd planned some sort of clandestine encounter. A meeting that required the cover of darkness."

I feel surprised once more, for how had such a simple line of reasoning not occurred to me? As soon as I arrived at Baskerville Hall, I'd become lost in its curious details. The original facts had been all but obscured.

"Yet what sort of meeting would require the master of the house such secrecy?" Holmes says. "I confess I was not sure until I located this." He holds up the ancient book, showing all of us the face of the many-eyed moon. "Herein lie the occult scribblings of the bringer of the so-called curse, Hugo Baskerville. For most of these pages, he describes in some detail his distasteful and obscure passions. But near the end, there's something more interesting. He explains the acts—or "offerings" as he calls them—that must be performed by future Baskervilles in order to hold what he calls the 'powers of darkness' at bay."

"Offerings?" Sir Henry says. "I've never heard of any such offerings."

"No," Holmes says. "Sir Charles was most certainly protecting you from such knowledge. As you've mentioned, you were his beloved cousin. And one does as one must for love."

I glance at Sir Henry and wonder if Holmes is implying the two baronets were involved in something more than a familial relationship.

"At any rate," Holmes continues. "Sir Charles went into the Yew Alley to make his sacrifice in accordance with an obscure date set in the Druidic calendar. But on this particular night of offering, he was ambushed by Mr. Perkins and his nephew, the young Mr. Barrymore."

"We did no such thing!" Perkins says.

Barrymore looks as if he's going to fall through the floor.

"At least one of them was in disguise," Holmes continues. "Dressed as a kind of punishing angel, come to—"

"Mr. Holmes," Barrymore says, voice trembling. "Please, sir. That's not what happened. You have it wrong."

"Quiet, boy!" Perkins yells.

But Barrymore won't be deterred. "You're in great danger here. You and Dr. Watson and Sir Henry. All of you."

"Mr. Holmes," Beryl Stapleton says. "I'm afraid the boy is correct. There is more to this than you might assume."

"That's what you'd have me believe, Miss Stapleton," Holmes says, turning toward her. "But I am well aware your name is not Beryl Stapleton. The actual woman of that name, a demure schoolmistress on holiday, perished nearly half a year ago in a fall upon the moor."

"It wasn't exactly a fall," she replies with a faint smile. "It was more of a..."

However, I do not hear the rest of her statement, for a shadow has appeared in the doorway behind Holmes.

It is the shape of a man. Very large. Nearly taller than the oaken frame.

It looms there. And before I can speak a warning, Holmes seems to sense it too, for he begins to turn. Yet even as he does, the dark presence takes him by the arm and, without hesitation, swings him quite suddenly and with vigorous force into the wall left of the door.

Holmes's face strikes the plaster with a loud crack.

There's a sound of breaking bone.

Sir Henry screams.

And as I stand from my chair, the figure swings Holmes back against the other wall, striking the crown of my old friend's head against it and leaving a smear of bright blood.

For a brief moment, Holmes meets my gaze, and there is a terrible look of shock on his face. He seems as if he wants me to acknowledge this is not the sort of thing that could happen. Certainly, there is some mistake.

His iconic nose is crooked, bloodied. His lower lip split. Even one of his teeth is missing.

The stranger—for it is the stranger who has come—swings him once again.

Holmes's feet skitter across the floor, trying to find purchase. But such struggle is of no use. His face strikes the wall a second time. And when Holmes is pulled back, his nose is nearly flattened. A large red welt obscures his left eye. And his expression is altered too. For the first time, he lacks a sense of knowing. His great intelligence appears to have drained away. And he stares dumbly at all of us as if he doesn't recognize these people or this place.

I grab a fireplace poker, the closest thing resembling a weapon, and charge. But before I can reach the dark figure, Holmes raises the pistol he clutches, and perhaps in some half-conscious bid for freedom, he fires it, not at the giant behind him, but into the parlor.

Sir Henry shrieks again. And I fear he's been shot.

When I turn, however, I see it's not the baronet who's been struck by Holmes's bullet but Dr. Mortimer. The doctor stands, looking at all of us, wide-eyed and slack-jawed in his well-made traveling suit. He has a rather large hole in the center of his forehead. A moment later, the doctor's knees fold, and he drops to the floor.

The figure in the doorway swings Holmes back and forth against the walls twice more, smashing his head vigorously into the plaster. Then he lets Holmes crumple onto the hardwood.

I stare at the body, expecting my old friend to rise and put an end to all this madness. But he remains quite motionless.

His regal neck is bent at an odd angle. A single gray eye peers out at us. And blood pools beneath him, soaking the folds of his Inverness cape.

As I look at him, a hollow and black chasm opens inside of me. Every touch of his hand. Every delicate kiss. All of it dripping down between the floorboards.

Baker Street too. Every adventure there has ever been.

I wonder if I am screaming. I wonder if I'm clutching at my own face.

But I do not have time to listen or feel. For now, the dark figure, dressed in the ancient red scraps of a military coat, steps over Holmes's body to enter the parlor.

One foot drags behind the other.

And though the oily lamplight pools upon the stranger's face, he remains as impossible to perceive as he was in the tower window.

Swollen yellow flesh and bulging eyes. Hair, a matted tangle.

There are features, yes. But they refuse to cohere.

I know what the face should look like. Of course, I do. I recognize its semblance from the painting of Hugo Baskerville in the portrait gallery. And yet this cannot be Hugo Baskerville. For that man has been dead some two hundred years or more. But here he stands before us, searching for something with his ruined eyes.

Then, Perkins scrambles forward like a rat and wrenches the bloodstained book from beneath Holmes's body.

"Dr. Watson, do not let my uncle have it!" Barrymore yells.

But it's too late, for Perkins has already opened the book and is reading aloud. Words I cannot understand. Phrases that have no sense about them.

And in the parlor, space itself grows stiff and strange.

Beryl Stapleton rises slowly from her chair. But she does not look like Beryl Stapleton any longer. It is as if she has been stretched. Long arms. And long legs. A towering head that nearly brushes the ceiling. She is the color of the smoke. No. She is the color of mist upon the moor. She is a striding thing. A figure that might have lived long ago and inspired fearful tales in Neolithic men.

Go, the striding thing says in a voice that is not a voice. All of you.

And before I know what I'm doing, I've taken Henry Baskerville and Barrymore by the hand. And because there is no other means of escape, we run toward the looming figure at the door.

# 19

The stranger waits for us, arms raised, fingers bent into claws, and even as I tell myself we are doomed, something incredible occurs—the parlor begins to shake. Dust sifts down from plaster moldings. Windows clatter in casements. Even the very floorboards start to shift.

I think of the trembling in the caves beneath the moor. The great black fissure. The roar inside my head. Have those otherworldly convulsions somehow reached the foundation of Baskerville Hall?

I hold onto Barrymore and Sir Henry, attempting to keep my balance.

The stranger in his tattered regalia sways like the mast of a storm-rocked ship. And though we draw near, he no longer fixes his rotted gaze upon us. Instead, he appears compelled by the words Perkins reads from the ancient book.

The old groom himself stands in a far corner of the room, chanting out a litany that, to my own ear, sounds as if it is spoken in some long-forgotten tongue.

What meaning does the stranger hear?

Is it the long-ago dreams of moorland men? Or a calling forth of spells? Or is it something more fantastic still?

Voice of the black fissure, tongue of darkness, reciting

truths no man has ever heard before. Secret geographies and hidden plateaus. The writhing of the Hound, a whine in its throat. And, of course, the souls of the boys of Grimpen Village forever pounding against the walls of fragile chests. Crying for release.

The striding thing that was once Beryl Stapleton shrieks as it moves through the trembling air of the parlor. Long-limbed. The color of mist. I catch a final glimpse of her as she raises the distended fingers of one awful gray hand, reaching for Perkins and the book.

Finally, the three of us reach the parlor door, and as I attempt to step over Holmes's broken body, my foot slips in his blood. A breath catches in my throat, and I find myself unable to move, staring down at my old friend's marble-like eye.

Barrymore turns and uses his considerable strength to pull me into the foyer.

Meanwhile, the trembling of the manor house has grown to a vigorous quake.

Sir Henry collapses, staring at a large crack forming in the wall above the wainscot.

Barrymore and I grab his arms and lift him, dragging the baronet onto the portico. Then the three of us are running, descending the stone steps, and moving out onto the cold moor.

Night has fallen.

A swollen yellow moon peers down at us with its many terrible eyes.

When we are some twenty paces from the portico, the house makes a new and deafening sound. A grinding and a howling. As if some invisible hand is twisting the entire structure, attempting to pull it from its foundation. And I know we must flee, but Sir Henry has turned and stares in stark horror at his ancestral home. “It’s moving,” he says breathlessly.

I do not understand his meaning until I turn and see for myself that Baskerville Hall appears to shift, slowly edging itself out onto the dark and heathered moor.

Such an image makes no sense to my eye. For a house cannot creep forth like some vast animal. And yet it does creep forth. Creaking and squealing. Pushing at the earth.

Windows on the second story shatter. Masonry breaks and falls.

I watch in horror as the southern tower begins to sway, slowly at first, then in widening arcs. It blots out the stars and the leering face of the moon.

Finally, there is a tremendous cracking sound, and the tower tips forward, falling like the arm of a dying man. It strikes the earth with terrible thunder.

The ground shakes beneath our feet.

And still, the house edges forth, relentless in its progress.

“The mire,” Sir Henry gasps. “It’s moving toward the Grimpen Mire.”

He’s right, of course. The great old house is impossibly shambling toward the bog.

I look to Barrymore, who stands behind us, staring in awe. And I wonder if he knew all along this would happen.

Was it part of the agreement with the creature? Another element in Perkins's plan?

"We're not safe here," Barrymore says. "They'll come for us. My uncle and his servant. We must go."

"Go where?" I ask.

"The standing stones. We'll be protected there. The Hound—"

At this, Sir Henry utters something between a moan and a scream. "I won't! That monster has plagued my family for centuries."

Barrymore puts a hand on Sir Henry's shoulder and looks hard into the baronet's eyes. "The only curse upon your house is the one my uncle brought. The Hound is innocent. I promise you."

Sir Henry looks again toward Baskerville Hall as the house crawls across the darkened fens, piling stone and earth on either side.

I take him by the arm. "We must do as Barrymore says."

He makes little sign of understanding, but at least he allows me to pull him along.

We follow Barrymore toward the standing stones. And as we grow near, I see the megalith is filled with rose-colored light. The glow of long-dead evenings. Bright mists of some ancient world. The standing stones are wrapped in flower garlands, black leaves, pale petals. And gathered there in the primordial haze are the figures I encountered days before, the men in leathers and women with flowers in their hair. They are bare-skinned. Lithe bodies dance or rest in beds of grass in numbers of three and four. They stroke and kiss one another, lost in passions, seemingly oblivious to the unnatural movements of the house. Or perhaps they are engaged in this way because of those movements.

Is this the true Grimpen Festival?

A final celebration. Death to an evil history.

My gaze is drawn toward the center of the megalith, to a shape that was, at first, hidden in the rose-colored mist. The creature itself is seated upon the stone altar: Hound of the Baskervilles. Decked in white garlands. Head of a dog. Body of a man. He lazes on the altar as if it is a throne, watching the orgy around him, pleased and tumescent. Flesh gleaming in the shifting light.

Despite the bizarre nature of the scene, I find I am not afraid.

For the rose-colored light soothes me.

And the movements of the men and women are like that of a hypnotist's pendulum.

I turn back to see the vast black shape of Baskerville Hall tipping forward into the Grimpen Mire. Stones fall. Columns break. The distant roar of a dying animal.

And a thought comes to me from far away: That is the grave of Sherlock Holmes. The grave of my old love.

When I turn back to the circle of standing stones, Barrymore is moving toward the altar. He strips off his shirt to reveal his hard, pale frame. Two of the celebrants approach him: a man with blond hair and a woman with red tresses. They help him with his boots and trousers.

Finally, he stands naked before the altar, drenched in the odd light of another world.

The celebrants wrap him in flower garlands.

And all the while, the Hound looks on, almost grinning, as if uplifted by the sight of an old friend.

Barrymore crawls onto the altar.

The Hound takes him by the hand, and when the creature leans forward to kiss Barrymore on the mouth, he is neither man nor dog but something in between. A form half composed of rose-colored light.

The Hound grasps Barrymore's stiffened cock, stroking it slowly.

Barrymore leans forward, kissing the Hound's thighs as a priest might kiss his holy vestments before a mass.

The Hound caresses Barrymore's cheek, and the boy presses forward to take the Hound's prodigious cock into his mouth. It throbs stiffly between his lips. And I understand it is not the cock of a man or a dog. It is instead the protection we seek.

As I watch, Barrymore sucks the great cock, moving his head slowly at first, then faster.

The Hound strokes Barrymore's dark hair with loving fondness.

Two celebrants are at my side, a man and a woman. They look at me with expectation. Another two stand beside Sir Henry. And when the baronet glances at me, I realize a healthy color has risen in him. It's as if he's seen something he was always meant to see.

His own personal god at work in its heaven.

I remove my suitcoat and unbutton my shirt while watching Barrymore with the Hound upon the altar.

The creature has lost its shape again, as it did when I first encountered it wandering in the mire.

It swells and contracts, enveloping the boy, caressing him everywhere at once.

And I am walking naked toward the altar with Sir Henry at my side.

Luminous tendrils reach for us.

Barrymore is on hands and knees, pale bottom raised. And the rose-colored light penetrates him slowly, deliberately. The light has a weight and a thickness. A cord of light. A shaft of light.

Barrymore throws back his head. And I am reminded that he is not merely some servant of the Baskervilles. He is the heir of Druid priests. Ages of power course through his veins.

Henry Baskerville climbs onto the altar to be cradled by the shapeless thing.

God of his house.

God of the moor.

A figure once worshipped by Neolithic men in this very circle of standing stones.

Sir Henry reclines and spreads his fair legs, and he too is penetrated by the light. It opens him. Fills him. The baronet moans with pleasure.

I look back once more to see the last of Baskerville Hall disappearing into the mire, sinking into the watery peat.

Soon it will be gone.

As it should be gone.

But I wonder about Perkins and the stranger. Did they escape? And if so, will they come for us? Can the Hound actually provide protection?

However, I do not have much time to consider such

questions, for I am led to the altar's edge by the celebrants. Toward Barrymore and Sir Henry and the Hound.

Then I climb onto the stone surface, surrounded by the rose-colored light.

Barrymore kisses me. I kiss him in return. Henry Baskerville takes my hand and holds it. Another presence is there with us too. A body that exists beyond hours and years, beyond the moor and even the Earth itself. It strokes me softly, licking my throat with a canid tongue.

I recline on the altar. The stone is not cold. It feels instead like a pool of warm water.

Barrymore is there beside me. And Henry Baskerville too. And my legs are gently parted as if by some cosmic hand. The dog and the man and the yellow moon above. There is something in all of this that makes me feel ready. As though I can be opened like a fissure in the earth. As though I am a fissure in the earth. Gaping and wanting. The tightly pulled knot of my history, my days with Sherlock Holmes, all untangling, releasing. Ever so slowly, a presence fills me. Thin at first like the mists upon the moor. Then swelling gradually, almost imperceptibly.

The Hound kisses me, and Barrymore sucks at my cock. And the rose-colored light, the Hound of the Baskervilles, is inside of me.

For the first time, my body allows such a thing as this.

There is no pain. Only strange joy.

And the pleasure is such that I am no longer merely myself. For the Hound is with me. And within me. Moving in and out. Slowly. Desirously.

And he does not feel alone. And I do not feel alone. And none of us there feel alone.

We are crying out all together. Eyes closed. For minutes and then hours. Until there is no time.

Finally, the Hound is spending inside of us. A hot voluminous flood.

Coming as only a god can come.

When I open my eyes, Barrymore, Sir Henry, and I are no longer on the altar in the circle of standing stones. Instead, we lie naked on what seems to be a wide, grassy plain.

Jagged, bone-white trees ring the edges of the plain.

The sky above is not blue but more a hazy rose.

And something like a moon hangs there. Yet it is not the moon. For I cannot name its shape or its color.

I look from Barrymore to Henry Baskerville. Their eyes are open, but they appear to be half inside a dream. I do not want to speak. Some part of me understands there is no reason to speak in a place like this. And yet another part (perhaps the one that worked with Sherlock Holmes for some twenty years) still feels I must ask a question. "Where are we?" I say softly.

Barrymore is slow to respond. When he finally does, his voice is distant. "A place that's safe."

"But what place?"

"Down in the chasm beneath the moor. Or..."

"Or what?"

"It's difficult to know. Difficult to say. But I think we might be inside of him. The Hound. Down in the light." Barrymore strokes the odd grass, and I realize it is not like grass at all but instead something akin to strange fur. "My mother used to tell me stories," he continues. "The spirits of the moor are vast. Bigger than the world when they need to be."

I study the curious white trees at the rim of the windless plain and briefly wonder if they might not look like jagged teeth.

I think of the Hound's gaping jaw. Is it possible we've been devoured?

Then I see creatures emerging from the wood. Luminous bodies like those I encountered in the caverns beneath the house. The creatures were lost in those bleak caves, blind and forlorn. But here they are at home. They gambol together, some flitting about on gossamer wings, others nibbling delicately at the fur-like grass.

"Look at them," Sir Henry says. He's propped himself up on his elbows to gaze at the creatures. "My God. Are they friendly, do you think?"

"They won't harm you, sir," Barrymore replies.

"This place," Sir Henry stands and turns in a slow circle. He's still entirely naked, but he seems not to notice. He wears an odd expression. It's something like joy. But there's madness in it too. For he is no longer burdened by the horrors of his inheritance. Having such a weight lifted so suddenly and completely must have been a great shock. "I dreamed of a place like this once," he says. "I wonder if Charlie dreamed it too."

"That would not surprise me, sir," Barrymore says. "You are Baskervilles, after all."

"Baskervilles," Sir Henry whispers as if this is some new and glorious word.

He looks up at the moon that is not a moon, and I briefly wonder if it might look like the golden eye of a watchful dog.

"I stayed in my room for such a very long time, you know," Sir Henry says. "I took so much medicine. Dram after dram. And I loved Charlie. My poor dear. I loved him so. But I slept for days... years. And what was I so afraid of?" He looks directly at me. "Dr. Watson, I think I shall go walking."

I nod as if granting some final and necessary permission. He turns slowly, moving off toward the strange animals, arms outstretched.

"Will Sir Henry recover?" I ask Barrymore.

"After a time, I should think." He holds his hand out to me. "Should we walk as well? I'd like to explore."

"You go ahead. I'm going to rest here for a bit. A brief moment to gather my thoughts."

"I'll see you soon then." He stands and begins to walk off toward the trees, not following Henry Baskerville but making his own path.

"Barrymore," I say.

When he turns to look at me, there's little left in him of the unsure young man I met upon my arrival at the house. He is free of his uncle. Free of Baskerville Hall. He stands before me now, a young magician, a Druid prince. And I realize he does not need my protection, my London. In fact, he might not need anything from me at all.

I smile and raise a hand.

He raises his own in return.

I am left in the fur-like grass, listening to the animals call to one another in curious voices.

# 20

How long do I lie there naked and alone beneath the watchful eye of the Hound?

Is it an hour? A day? Or more like a century?

In truth, I do not know. For this hermetic plain makes something new of time.

(A house unbuilt. A landscape glimpsed only through the milk-white lens of dreams.)

And what thoughts do I think as I stretch my limbs in the prickling grass? As I feel the lightness of my own body. The place where he entered me. Where he was with me. Dog that is not a dog. Man that is not a man. What exactly did he spill inside of me?

A rosy sky?

Trees like teeth?

Is this what Hugo Baskerville wanted so many years ago? Did he, too, wish for fields of halcyon?

Mysterium Tremendum. Mystery as Revelation.

We are not so different, you and I. Come, let me break your bones.

Yet I am not broken. He has not broken me. Nor have the years. Nor any world. I know this. I recognize it here in the quiet golden field. And perhaps this recognition is what leads me back to the face of Sherlock Holmes.

For despite my love, was he not the greatest of the breaking wheels?

I do not picture the mask of confusion he wore in the parlor. I cannot bear to think of the blood and horror. Instead, another mask emerges. Candlelit, serene.

It is the handsome face Holmes wore during our first dinner together.

He invited me to Marcini's. I still looked like a soldier then. Square-shouldered. Ruddy cheeked. And Holmes himself was lean and strong from his nights in the boxing ring.

He smiled at me that evening, thin-lipped, reclining in his chair. And he told me a story about a case he'd solved during college. It was the first of his adventures I was ever to encounter. And as I listened, I thought I had never heard anything quite so fine. The way he moved me through the careful steps of the investigation allowed me to see and yet not quite see ... elementary ... elementary ....

I remember leaning against the table in the dim-lit dining room, resting my arms upon the tablecloth.

I must have looked like a boy delighted.

And when Holmes came to the climax of his tale, he did something so utterly surprising. An act I could not quite believe. He reached out and brushed his thin fingers lightly over the knuckles of my left hand.

It happened so quickly. I'm sure no one else in the restaurant even took note.

But for me, it was as if some great lever had been thrown, and the energy of a vast, hidden machine suddenly crackled down through the atmosphere, raining upon us.

Of course, I'd known other men—in paneled dormitories and army barracks, foul rooms over Piccadilly, and even in the overgrown and secret shadows of Regent's Park.

Yet this simple touch was something so much more than all of that.

Maybe it was because of the story Holmes had told, or the rich flavor of the roasted duck, or the way the Great Detective gazed at me. Whatever the reason, Marcini's dazzled around us. Brilliant damask and blazing silver. White tablecloths like islands in a shimmering sea.

And as I drew my hand back from the table, a revelation wrote itself large in the delicate pages of my heart: it is possible to fall in love.

And I knew at that moment this would not be the love described by our fathers and mothers, the love asserted by the age.

No. This love would be a daring thing, as bold as the new century.

I was going to make a house with this man. I'd accompany him through foggy streets, keeping track of his brilliant affairs. Then I'd lay with him at night, kiss him, and sleep in his strong embrace. And in the early morning hours, when the breakfast fires burned, I'd write out our adventures, step by careful step, as if recording the greatest of all medical miracles. A process of healing unparalleled.

I'd show everyone how remarkable Holmes was. And I would be remarkable in return.

I believed all of that.

And now, as I gaze up at the rose-colored sky, I understand all my old truths have come undone. Marcini's, Baker Street, and even London itself are nothing more than painted scrims. And Holmes is dead. Impossibly dead.

I ask myself, what is left here in this field of grass? This place that is not a place.

The Hound gave me solace, yes, but not understanding.

What am I that rests upon the plain?

## 21

Soon a flickering light appears in the forest at the edge of the golden field. It is not one of the luminous creatures. For this presence does not amble. It moves instead with purpose. I feel drawn to it. Beckoned.

I stand carefully and make my way toward the trees. It's there in the jagged wood I find her, Beryl Stapleton, dressed in what might be the linen garments of a maiden, hair woven into a loose braid. She looks almost like a peasant girl from an old woodcut. Almost I say because there is something so unusual about the garment as if each thread pulses with a curious radiance. She might just as well be dressed as a figure from some distant future. A new Romantic age where clothes and morals no longer bind.

She's gazing at one of the luminous animals, a small thing like a dragonfly, except it, has long, jointed legs and a face with pale, inquisitive eyes. The insect returns her gaze almost sweetly. Under one arm, she holds Hugo Baskerville's tattered book. She glances up at me. And it's only at that moment I remember I am naked. Yet I do not feel ashamed. I wonder briefly if I've gone half-mad like Henry Baskerville. But it's more than that, I think. Something about this place makes me feel as though I should be naked. As if we are all meant to be so.

"Dr. Watson," Beryl Stapleton says pleasantly as if we are old acquaintances who've spotted each other on a London street corner. "You look as though you're feeling better."

I clear my throat. "It's rather more complicated than that, I should say."

"Is it?" she asks.

I do not know exactly how to answer her question—and there is a part of me that remains very much afraid of Beryl Stapleton—so instead of replying directly, I gesture toward the book. "What of Perkins?"

She sighs. "He put up a good fight for such an old man. A surprising amount of blood in the end. All of it his, of course."

"He's dead?"

"I tore off his jaw and fed it to him." She reaches out and attempts to pet the dragonfly. It makes an irritated, buzzing sound and flutters off into the rosy sky. "He wouldn't give me what I wanted. But I suppose I would have killed him anyway. He'd grown too powerful, as priests and augurs sometimes do."

"And the other one ... the stranger?"

She tilts her head. "Why do you insist on calling him that? You know very well who it was."

"Such things," I say, "they should not exist."

"Hence my constant toiling," she strokes the braid of her hair. "The stranger, as you would have it, will wander, I suppose, as wayward phantoms do. Farmers and secret lovers will be frightened from time to time by his bleak shadow on the moor. Stories will be repeated around the hearths of Devon. But he poses no real threat. Not without this."

She pats the yellow book. And when I do not immediately respond—perhaps because I am thinking of my walks upon the moor when I too appeared as a kind of shade—she reaches out and touches my bare arm. Her skin feels not like skin at all. It is something far colder. A stone from the ruins at the end of the world. "I'm sorry about Sherlock Holmes," she says.

I find I am startled by the sound of his name. And I wonder if there will be tears. But there are none. Not yet, at least. "I was just thinking of him."

"And what were you thinking?"

I shake my head. "It's difficult to explain."

"Please try," she says. "It's not often I ask to hear about someone's feelings, you know."

I take a breath. "I suppose I thought I told so many of our stories. Years of them. But they weren't our stories at all."

"Who did they belong to then?" Beryl Stapleton says.

"No one, it seems to me now. No one at all." I wipe at my tearless eyes and look again at her country dress. I picture the gray mist, the long limbs, the voice that seemed to echo from everywhere at once. "When I saw you in the parlor. You became—what exactly are you?"

She glances off into the woods as if she heard something moving there. "I thought you might have guessed by now. Then again, detective work, you know. I'm afraid I don't have time to play games of truth today."

"But—"

"I still have a job to finish. Would you like to attend?"

"Is it far?" I ask.

"No. Not far. Just over there." She gestures toward the trees.

*

We walk in the woods together, stepping over fallen white branches. The curious animals observe our progress. Their pale eyes. Their open mouths. "They are quite lovely, aren't they?" Beryl Stapleton says. "Gentle sylph-like things. It's been a long while since I've walked here."

"Is this your home?"

"This? Oh no. Nothing so bucolic."

"Where then, if I might ask?"

She smiles a vague sort of smile and, taking my hand, pulls me gently toward the edge of the wood. When we emerge from the tree line, I expect to see yet another grassy plain or perhaps a far-off village. But instead, we stand upon a rocky precipice. And beyond the precipice is nothing but the rose-colored light. A great wall of light. Churning and flickering. As if the air has been set on fire. There's something else too. A distant sound. Not a hushing or a trembling like the noise that came from the fissure beneath the moor. This is almost its opposite: a bright cacophony. Like a thousand voices, all calling out from the glittering rooms of some distant celebration.

"What is this place?" I ask, gazing into the light.

"The edge of things, I suppose we might say."

"Edge?"

"Do you know why I took such an interest in you when we first met in the natatorium?" Beryl Stapleton asks.

I shake my head.

"Because you seemed unfinished. And I have always preferred unfinished things."

I turn to see her eyes are filled with an emotion I cannot begin to comprehend.

"To solve a mystery is to destroy it, Dr. Watson," she says. "And that is the same as destroying life. You have never solved a mystery, have you?"

"I have not," I say honestly.

"Very good. That's very good indeed." She opens the book and takes the first rotting page that Hugo Baskerville penned some two hundred years before, tearing it free from its ancient bindings. Then without ceremony, she tosses the page into the rose-colored light. It does not fall but seems instead to fade from view as if swallowed slowly.

"Would you like to help me?" she asks, offering the book.

I reach down and tear out the second page. It feels soft, like calfskin. I hold it delicately as I step toward the precipice, wondering if I should look at the words scrawled upon it. But I realize I have no need. I already understand what these pages contain. Dark hallways. Rooms without meaning. All of it repeating over and again.

I stand at the edge of the precipice, and with a careful hand, I gently release the page. It flutters there in the rosy light. Burning, dissolving. Finally free.

"Miss Stapleton," I whisper. For there are many questions, I want to ask. And she is the sort who would know the answers. I realize that now. I should have been asking her all along.

But there is no response.

There's only the burning sky and the sound of the distant celebration.

*

When I turn to look for her, it's not Beryl Stapleton I find, but the shadows of Barrymore and Sir Henry moving through the trees. I enter the pale forest and call to them. They turn toward me, naked still, looking ever so vital. There's a sheepish expression on both of their faces.

"Finally," Barrymore says. "We were searching for ages, John."

"Were you?" I ask, feeling pleased someone would take the time to look for me.

"We thought we might try to find a way out of here," Barrymore says. "We can't stay forever, you know. It's not that sort of place."

"No," I say, glancing down at a weird colorless beetle with all-too-human eyes that trundles through the underbrush. "I suppose it's not. Have you devised a plan?"

"I understand a few things about these matters," Barrymore runs his fingers through his dark hair. "I talked it over with Sir Henry, and, well, we thought we might try fucking."

I blink in surprise. Then I look at Sir Henry, imagining the baronet might raise some protest. But he merely nods, appearing pleased. "That is what we decided, Dr. Watson," he says.

"It's an experiment, of course," Barrymore continues. "But that is how we got here, isn't it? And there's something about this place that makes the idea seem like—well, it might be fun."

I stare at them a moment longer, and I begin to smile. I cannot stop smiling at the ridiculousness of this suggestion. Then I am laughing too. "An experiment," I say. "Really?"

"A very good one, I should think," Sir Henry says, clapping me on the back. "Possibly quite pleasurable."

"Well, I suppose it's worth a try, isn't it?" I say.

"Multiple tries perhaps," Barrymore says, putting his arms around us.

"There's probably no wrong way to do it," Sir Henry adds.

"No," I say. "Probably no wrong way at all."

And as we make our way through the bright forest, searching for some grassy bed, Barrymore begins to sing a cheerful song.

At first, I think it is a tune I recognize. Something from a very long time ago. The war. Or my childhood. But I realize I'm mistaken.

I've never heard this song before.

Soon enough, though, we are all singing along.

# Acknowledgements:

I am forever grateful to Steve Berman for fighting the good fight in the world of queer literature. At Lethe Press, Steve provides a home for so many titles that might go otherwise unacknowledged and unseen. I'd also like to extend thanks to my colleagues and students at Vermont College of Fine Arts who consistently remind me of the wide and dynamic range of possibilities in fiction. Thank you to Brian Leung for reading many drafts of my work over the years and responding with intelligence, humor, and compassion. For their help with my writing and for their continued friendship, I'd like to thank Chris Baugh, Christine Sneed, Scott Blindauer, and Gabriel Blackwell. Thank you also to my supportive mother and father, Denise and Michael, and my sisters, Sarah and Elizabeth. And finally, thank you to the amazing and ravishingly handsome Brad Gilmore who provides romance and sweet levity at every turn here in the dim strange streets of Los Angeles.

# About the Author

Adam McOmber is the author of three novels, *The White Forest, Jesus and John,* and *The Ghost Finders,* as well as three collections of short stories: *My House Gathers Desires, This New & Poisonous Air* and *Fantasy Kit.* He is a core faculty member in the Writing Program at Vermont College of Fine Arts as well as editor-in-chief of the literary magazine *Hunger Mountain.*

www.ingramcontent.com/pod-product-compliance
Ingram Content Group UK Ltd.
Pitfield, Milton Keynes, MK11 3LW, UK
UKHW041951190726
13854UKWH00005B/1910

9 781590 215197